DEATH RIDES THE RAILS

Center Point
Large Print

Also by James J. Griffin and available from
Center Point Large Print:

Death Stalks the Rangers

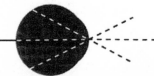

DEATH RIDES THE RAILS

A Texas Ranger Jim Blawcyzk Story

James J. Griffin

CENTER POINT LARGE PRINT
THORNDIKE, MAINE

This Center Point Large Print edition
is published in the year 2017 by arrangement with
the author.

Copyright © 2012 by James J. Griffin.

This is a much-altered version of the previously published
book *Trouble Rides the Texas Pacific*.

This is a work of fiction.
All names, characters, places, and events are the work
of the author's imagination. Any resemblance to real
persons, places, or events is coincidental.

The text of this Large Print edition is unabridged.
In other aspects, this book may vary
from the original edition.
Printed in the United States of America
on permanent paper.
Set in 16-point Times New Roman type.

ISBN: 978-1-68324-520-9

Library of Congress Cataloging-in-Publication Data

Names: Griffin, James J., 1949– author.
Title: Death rides the rails : a Texas Ranger Jim Blawcyzk story /
   James J. Griffin.
Description: Center Point Large Print edition. | Thorndike, Maine :
   Center Point Large Print, 2017.
Identifiers: LCCN 2017024369 | ISBN 9781683245209
   (hardcover : alk. paper)
Subjects: LCSH: Texas Rangers—Fiction. | Large type books.
Classification: LCC PS3607.R5477 D427 2017 | DDC 813/.6—dc23
LC record available at https://lccn.loc.gov/2017024369

In memory of my mother, Ruth,
and father, Willis

CHAPTER ONE

"Conductor, I insist you tell me why this train is being delayed. *Immediately!*"

In vain, a flustered Mike Hardy, chief conductor on the Texas and Pacific's Shreveport-El Paso Limited, looked around the crowded Dallas station platform for help.

"I'm sorry, Miz . . ."

"It's Mrs. Mrs. Isaac Hollister," the middle-aged matron snapped. She waggled her finger under his nose. "I demand to know when we'll be on our way."

"As I've already explained, Mrs. Hollister," the harried conductor replied, "I really don't know any more than you. I can only tell you we have orders to wait for the local from Austin, and it's late. There's a passenger on that train who must make his connection with this one. I checked with the station agent a few minutes ago, and he assured me the Austin train will be here within a half-hour. Once it arrives and the passenger transfers, we will be on our way, I assure you."

Mrs. Hollister harrumphed. "We had better be, young man. I assure *you* that I shall make a formal complaint to the president of this railroad, the moment I reach El Paso."

"Yes, ma'am," Hardy replied. "In the meantime,

why don't you return to your car? You'll be more comfortable there, away from the wind and soot."

As if to punctuate his words, the engine lurched forward several feet, sending cinders spewing from its smokestack.

"I'll return to my seat, but don't you dare think you're fooling me. Not for one minute. I know when I'm being given the runaround. Make no mistake about that."

"Yes, ma'am." Hardy helped the woman up the coach steps and heaved a sigh as she disappeared inside. When he stepped back, engineer Chip Danvers swung down from the cab of his locomotive, a wide grin splitting his red-bearded face.

"Saw that woman givin' you what-for, Mike. Figured a nice soot shower would send her back to her seat so I hit the throttle, just a bit. What the devil was she complainin' about?"

"About us runnin' so late, Chip. What else? Can't say as I blame her."

Danvers mimicked the indignant matron. "I can just hear her now. I demand to know when we're departing. I know when I'm being given the runaround, young man. No reason for her to take her mad out on you, though."

"Not you too, Chip. Sheesh," the frustrated conductor retorted. He pulled his watch from his vest and glanced at it. "We're already two hours late pulling out of here. Do you hear me? Two hours. It's enough to make a man cuss. Dadblast it all anyway."

"Do you know anything about this character we're waiting for?" Danvers asked.

"Not a thing. All I know is we've been ordered to hold this train for him, no matter what. Had to hook that blasted cattle car onto the Limited, too. Whoever heard of adding a cattle car to a crack passenger train? Anyhow, those orders came straight from company headquarters. Dadblast whoever issued 'em."

"Well, whoever it is, he must be some high and mighty muckety-muck, to hold up a fast express like the Limited," Danvers said. "I'm sure eager to lay my eyes on him."

The lonesome sound of a distant train whistle came from down the tracks toward Austin.

"Looks like you'll get your chance pretty quick," Hardy said. Here comes the Austin local, and none too soon." He pulled out his watch again. "And only two hours and thirty seven minutes late."

Hardy and Danvers, along with the Limited's other crewmen and several of its passengers, watched curiously as the ancient, wood-burning locomotive pulling the Austin-Dallas local huffed into the station, billowing steam and smoke, then ground to a halt. They stared intently at the passengers alighting from the coaches, becoming

9

even more puzzled as every passenger headed into the depot, or to waiting buggies and hacks.

"Mebbe we waited for nothing." Danvers said, tugging on his beard.

"Well, if we did, I'm gonna make sure someone's head rolls," Hardy snapped. "I'm goin' to talk to the agent. Right now."

"Hold it just a minute, Mike." Danvers put a hand on the conductor's arm when one last passenger came around the back of the local. "Betcha' this is our man."

"Him? Can't be. He's just a driftin' cowpoke," Hardy said.

The cowboy was in his late twenties or early thirties, a shade over six feet tall, and wore a tan Stetson, under which a fringe of shaggy blonde hair could be seen. His deep blue eyes seemed to take in everything, and everyone, on the platform. He wore ordinary range garb, a faded blue shirt topped off by a red bandanna tied loosely around his neck, a leather vest, worn denim pants, and scuffed boots. An 1873 Colt Peacemaker, still rare in Texas, hung from his left hip.

However, what really captured the trainmen's notice was the horse the cowboy led. The palomino and white-splotched paint gelding was anything but ordinary. His coat gleamed, even under the covering of soot from his ride in a boxcar attached to the local. The horse pranced proudly, neck arched. He nuzzled his rider's shoulder impatiently as they approached the waiting trainmen.

"Evenin', gents." The cowboy touched the brim of his hat in a brief salute. "This the El Paso Limited?"

"It sure is, Mister," Hardy replied. "You the jasper we're holdin' this train for?"

"Reckon I am. Name's Jim Blawcyzk."

"Bluahw . . . huh?"

"BLUH-zhick. It's Polish, but Jim'll do just fine," the cowboy said, with a friendly twinkle in his eyes. "This here's Sam."

He indicated the horse, who laid his ears back and made as if to lunge at Hardy.

"Easy, fella," Jim said. "Sorry. Sam's pretty much a one-man horse. We've been trail pards for some years."

"I can see that," Danvers said, dryly. "I'm Chip Danvers, the engineer on this run, and this is Mike Hardy, the conductor."

"Nice to meet you fellas. And I appreciate your holdin' the train for me."

"We didn't have any choice," Hardy grumbled, the frown still on his face. "The sooner you get aboard, the sooner we can get movin'. We've got to make up plenty of lost time."

"Sure," Jim agreed. A wide, crooked smile crinkled his face. "I'll have Sam settled in a jiffy."

Hardy and Danvers gave Jim's broad back a

11

bewildered stare as he led his horse to the cattle car.

"Can't figure why we'd hold the train for someone like that," Hardy muttered in disgust.

"Me neither," Danvers agreed, "But that horse of his is really somethin'." He turned away. "Well, I'd better have Suggs start building the fire back up, so we can get rollin'. See you in Mineral Wells, Mike."

Danvers climbed back into the engine's cab.

The paint snorted a protest as he climbed the ramp and lunged into the cattle car.

"Easy, Sam," Jim soothed him. "You should be enjoyin' this, a nice easy ride on a train, rather'n havin' to carry me three hundred miles."

As Jim uncinched the saddle and lifted it from Sam's back, the gelding nuzzled insistently at his back pocket.

"All right, here's your candy," Jim laughed, as he dug in his pocket and came up with a peppermint, which Sam eagerly took. "Last one until we get off the train," Jim scolded. He carefully placed his saddle in a corner, making sure the Winchester in its scabbard was free and clear. That done, he slipped the bridle from Sam's head, replaced it with a halter, and tied Sam's lead to a support post, making sure there was enough rope so the horse could move about freely. Sam buried his muzzle in some sweet-smelling hay, and his rider slapped him fondly on the shoulder.

"That's right, chow down while you've got the chance," Jim said, then chuckled. "I'll be just a couple cars ahead of you."

Sam raised his head and whickered softly.

Jim reassured him. "Don't worry, I'll check on you every stop." With a final pat to the horse's nose, Jim stepped from the car, bolted the door shut, and hurried to his coach. Mike Hardy bellowed his "All Aboard!" and the big drivers on the locomotive started to turn as the Ranger clambered into the car.

Jim found a seat against the rear bulkhead of the coach, where he could see anyone who came in or left, and didn't have to expose his back. Most of the seats were empty anyway, the car less than half-full. He tipped his Stetson in greeting to the woman and a wide-eyed girl of about six, probably her daughter, who occupied the seats across the aisle. The little girl returned his grin with a shy smile. Couplers clanked and steam hissed. As the train lurched into motion, Jim settled his lean frame into the seat, adjusted the gunbelt around his waist, stretched out his legs, and tilted his hat over his eyes. One thing a Ranger learned, and fast, was to grab sleep whenever he could.

With a long sigh, Jim closed his eyes. Truth to tell, he didn't care for the train any more than his horse did. He'd much rather be on horseback, crossing the rolling Texas plains in the fresh air, instead of riding in this noisy, cramped, soot-spewing, foul-smelling contraption. But in the unincorporated areas of the Panhandle, friction was growing between ranchers and homesteaders. New counties were being organized, and the competition among communities vying to be county seats was fierce. Several candidates for public office had been threatened with violence. Local law was limited to the scattered settlements, so Ranger assistance had been requested. Captain Hank Trumbull, Jim's commanding officer, had ordered him to reach the territory as quickly as possible. Given the choice of a week's hard riding or a fifteen hour train ride, Jim, after much protesting, reluctantly agreed to let Trumbull pull some strings and arrange passage for himself and Sam from Dallas to Sweetwater on the El Paso Limited. From Sweetwater, he still faced three days on horseback to the budding community which would eventually be incorporated as Lubbock, then he and Sam would move on into the upper Texas Panhandle. While the train raced along at thirty miles per hour, Jim allowed himself to be lulled to sleep by the rhythmic clicking of the rails beneath the wheels.

The El Paso Limited made a brief stop in Mineral Wells, where Jim checked on Sam while the train took on water for the engine's boiler and picked up a few more passengers. The train soon resumed its westward journey, and as it climbed slowly through the rugged Palo Pinto Mountains, Jim once again drifted off to sleep.

". . . James Joseph Blawcyzk! The last dance is coming up, and you'll be dancing it with me!" Jim's petite wife's brown eyes shone with mock indignation. Jim, Julia and their eight year old son, Charlie, were at the St. Cecelia's Roman Catholic Church, their home parish's, annual dance and social. The tall Ranger was far from the handsomest man at the gathering, but he did have rugged good looks, was also a good dancer, and enjoyed it immensely. No wonder then, he was a popular partner with most of the ladies.

"Yes'm," Jim replied softly, answering her mock glare with a crooked grin. "You know I always save the last dance for you, darlin'."

"Don't worry, Julia, I'm not going to steal your husband," Maria Justus, Julia's best friend and wife of San Leanna sheriff Tom Justus, assured her, laughing. "Thank you for the dance, Jim. I'd better go round up Tom. I'm sure he's outside having

15

a swallow from the jug Ben Fredricks brought."

"The pleasure was all mine," Jim replied.

"That's enough flirting, Jim," Julia ordered. When the three-piece band, consisting of fiddle, guitar, and harmonica, commenced playing "Skip to My Lou" Jim took her in his arms, brushing a lock of Julia's brunette hair back from her forehead as he swept her onto the dance floor. Julia smiled up at her husband while they whirled across the room. She knew his love and loyalty for her knew no bounds, and his dancing with the other women was just that, and nothing more. The only jealousy she ever felt was for Jim's other love, the Texas Rangers. Julia had long known that, while she could fight off any female who tried for her husband, she'd always have to share him with the Rangers. His long and frequent absences only made their time together that much sweeter.

The next dance was a lively version of "Get Along Home, Little Cindy," followed by the traditional final number, "Good Night, Ladies." After making their goodbyes, Jim and Julia rounded up Charlie, who'd spent most of the

16

night playing tag with his friends. While Charlie, whose blue eyes and blonde hair made him the spitting image of his father, climbed into the back of the buckboard, Jim and Julia settled onto the wagon's seat. Jim clucked to Ben and Jerry, the team of matched draft horses, to start them on the short trip home.

Curled up under a blanket, Charlie was soon asleep. Julia snuggled close to Jim while the horses trotted along.

"Happy, Julia?" Jim asked.

"You know I am," Julia whispered. "I only wish you didn't have to leave again so soon."

"Well, you could've done a lot better'n marryin' a fiddle-footed Texas Ranger. Bet a hat on that," Jim replied.

"But I love that fiddle-footed Texas Ranger," Julia answered. As she reached up to kiss his cheek, a coyote's howl startled the team. The horses broke into a gallop, then a dead run. Jim hauled back on the reins, frantically attempting to stop the runaway horses. When the team raced into a sharp curve, the buckboard slewed sideways, tilting on two wheels . . .

Jim jerked awake as the train coach tilted upward, jouncing roughly across the tracks. This was no dream. Couplers crashed together, and metal wheels screeched on metal rails when the engineer slammed on the brakes. The little girl who had smiled at Jim was tossed against the seat in front of her as the car jerked and bucked. The coach tipped even more, and she toppled into the aisle.

Jim jumped to his feet, intending to grab the child, but the derailing coach telescoped into the car ahead. It listed at a sickening angle, and Jim flew across the aisle; his head slammed into the metal edge of a seat. The car turned on its side: wood splintered and tortured metal screamed as it plowed along the roadbed. Stunned, protected from even greater injury by his Stetson, Jim was unable to move quickly enough to avoid a heavy cross brace that ripped from its moorings and smashed into his ribs. The doomed train finally shuddered to a halt, and Jim Blawcyzk lay motionless in the destroyed coach.

CHAPTER TWO

The awful grinding of tortured metal, splintering wood, and shattering glass ended, replaced momentarily by an eerie silence, punctuated only by the hiss of escaping steam. Then the pungent odor of spilled coal oil, the cries of injured passengers, and the crackling of flames roused Jim back to his senses. The ceiling lamps had fallen from their brackets and smashed, spilling their fuel. The kerosene ignited as it spread throughout the car. Flames licked eagerly at the oil-soaked wood.

Struggling to pull air into his tortured lungs, Jim shoved aside the jagged beam that lay across his ribs and forced himself upright. Sharp pain stabbed through his side when he came to his feet. He swayed dizzily as he tried to keep his balance.

A quick glance around the coach showed several passengers were beyond help. Others were struggling to their feet or pulling themselves along on hands and knees, trying to escape the flaming wreckage. Jim dragged himself over the jumbled debris which covered the side of the car, which was now in effect the floor. He climbed over twisted seats and ripped-open luggage, to where the girl who'd smiled shyly at him was sitting alongside her mother. She was sniffling. Her mother lay pinned under a seat, unconscious, a livid bruise beginning to show on her forehead.

"What's your name, honey?" Jim asked. He smiled to reassure the child.

"It's . . . Sarah," she managed to say through her sniffles. "My mommy's hurt."

"I'm Jim," he said. "Don't worry, I'll have you and your mom out of here in a jiffy. "You'll both be just fine."

He grasped the seat that trapped the woman, muttering in frustration when it refused to budge. Pain shot through his ribs. He'd need help.

"I'll be right back, Sarah. I just need to find someone to help me lift this seat. You stay with your mom until I get back. Promise?"

"I promise." Sarah nodded in agreement.

Thick smoke was rapidly filling the wrecked car. It burned Jim's lungs and throat and blurred his vision as he looked around the coach. To his dismay, the remaining passengers had already fled, abandoning their fellow travelers to the rapidly spreading flames.

A moan that seemed to come from just beyond another pile of rubble caught Jim's attention. He scrambled over the debris to find a young cowboy lying with his legs pinned under a thick beam.

The cowpuncher caught sight of the Ranger.

"Help me outta here, mister," he pleaded. "I think my leg's busted."

"Just a minute," Jim replied. He pulled his bandanna over his mouth and nose to filter out some of the choking smoke. "If I lift the beam, can you drag yourself outta there?"

"You bet I can," the cowboy answered. "Just get that blasted thing offa me."

"Okay," Jim said. "Get ready." He grasped one end of the beam, and his muscles bunched under his shirt as he strained to lift it and free the trapped man. Creaking, the splintered wood shifted ever so slightly.

"Now! Slide outta there," Jim ordered, then bit his lips against the pain in his ribs as he kept the beam from dropping back. The cowboy shoved himself backward, out from under the beam.

"Thanks, mister," he gasped.

Jim let his breath gush out as he released the heavy beam. "Don't mention it," he said. "Come on. We've gotta hurry."

The cowboy attempted to rise, but collapsed with a groan when his right leg couldn't take his weight.

"Guess it . . . really is busted," he gritted. "Better leave me and get outta here, mister, before it's too late."

"Not a chance," Jim snapped. "I'm not abandoning you, and leavin' you here to roast. Besides, I need your help to get a woman and her little girl out of this car. Just lean on me, and we'll get out. Bet a hat on it."

"Sure. Sure, mister," the cowboy agreed. "I don't much hanker to fry like Sunday's chicken anyway."

"Save your breath." Jim draped the cowboy's arm over his shoulders, lifted him to his feet, and helped the injured man over the rubble which had trapped him.

Sarah still waited alongside her injured mother, just like she promised Jim. His eyes widened with concern when he saw how rapidly the flames had spread. Carefully, he lowered the cowboy to where he could grasp the upended seat that pinned the unconscious woman.

"I told you I'd be right back, Sarah," Jim said. "This is . . ."

"Pete," the cowboy said.

"Pete," Jim echoed. "And you remember my name, don't you?"

"Jim," Sarah replied, her voice barely above a whisper. Her lips trembled and tears rolled down her cheeks.

"That's right," Jim said. He smiled, then wedged his boots under the seat. "Now, we're gonna get you and your mom out of here."

He looked at Pete, who had braced his shoulder against the bottom of the seat. The cowboy's face was white and taut with pain.

"You ready?" Jim asked.

"As much as I can be," Pete replied. "Just give the word."

"Now!" Jim rammed both his legs upward as Pete pushed hard against the bench. Both men grunted with the effort. Finally, with a wrenching protest, the seat moved, just a bit.

"Get her out from under there, Jim," Pete shouted. "I'm not sure how long I can hold it."

Jim scrambled to his knees and jerked the woman free. Pete let the seat fall back into place.

"She still alive?" he asked.

"So far." Jim noted the woman's shallow, but steady, breathing. "But none of us will be for long it we don't find a way out of here."

Both exits from the coach were blocked, the front one smashed when the car telescoped into the lead coach, the other now sealed off by the rapidly spreading conflagration. Jim glanced at the windows overhead.

"Pete, if I push you through one of those windows, can you lift Sarah and her mother out of here?"

"Count on it," Pete replied. "So stop jawin' and get at it."

Jim levered himself to his feet and pulled his Colt from its holster. He jerked the bandanna from his face and wrapped it around the gun, then used the Peacemaker's barrel to smash jagged shards of glass from one of the windows. That done, he helped Pete to his feet, grasped the cowboy around the waist, and lifted him to the window. Pete strained with the effort as he pulled himself out of the coach, then twisted and lay on his belly. He reached for Sarah when Jim lifted the girl to him.

"My mommy!" Sarah cried, as Jim pushed her into Pete's grasp.

"Don't worry. She'll be with you in a minute," Jim assured her. "You just do what Pete says."

"Jim's right," Pete soothed the six-year old. He pulled her through the window and placed her alongside him. "Don't move, honey," he told her. "Just wait, and your mom'll be with you in a minute. You got the woman, Jim?"

"I've got her," Jim called back. Battling the pain in his ribs, his throbbing head, and the thick, asphyxiating smoke, he wrestled with the woman's dead weight and lifted her up. As he felt the last of his strength about to give out, Pete pulled the woman from his grip, yanking her outside. A moment later, the cowboy's smoke-blackened face reappeared at the window.

"C'mon, Jim. You ain't got time to dawdle around," he urged.

"I've gotta try to get these other folks outta here," Jim answered. "Can't just leave 'em."

"Jim, you can't do anything for them," Pete snapped. "And I sure can't get these folks off this car without your help. Come on!"

"I guess you're right," Jim reluctantly agreed.

A tongue of flame shot across the car. The soles of his boots were smoldering. He stretched up his arms and allowed Pete to grab his wrists. Wincing at the pain tearing through his side, Jim pulled himself up and out of the burning car. He rolled onto his back, gratefully gulping huge draughts of relatively cool, fresh air.

"We've gotta get down off here, Jim, and right quick," Pete urged. Flames now shot out of the car's shattered windows.

"Gimme a minute," Jim said. He rolled onto his stomach, then pushed himself to his hands and knees. Choking, fighting the nausea that churned his belly and the vertigo that threatened to overcome him, he crawled to the edge of the derailed coach.

A quick glance through the swirling smoke revealed a scene of utter pandemonium. Passengers and crewmen raced to pull trapped or incapacitated people from the crushed cars. A number of the injured had already been moved some distance from the wrecked train. Their groans mixed with the crackling of the flames, the hiss of steam, and the frantic cries of the rescuers. Leaning over the edge of the coach, Jim called to a brakeman who was rushing past.

"Hey, up here! I need a hand gettin' some folks offa this car."

"Be right with you," the brakeman shouted back. "Just let me find another pair of hands."

He ran to a group of men pulling injured riders from the next coach, grabbed one by the shoulder and whirled him around, then pointed to Jim's precarious perch. A moment later, both men were standing directly below the Ranger.

"We're ready." The brakeman shouted to be heard over the roaring fire. "How many you got up there?"

"Three besides me," Jim replied. "A little girl and her mother, who's unconscious, plus a cowpoke with a broken leg. I'll have to lower them down to you."

"You'd better hurry," the brakeman urged. "The fire's spreading fast. What's left of that car might collapse under you any minute."

Pete appeared at Jim's side.

"Brought the ladies over, Jim," he grunted. Somehow, despite his injuries, Pete had managed to drag the unconscious woman to the edge of the car.

"Thanks, Pete," Jim said, then turned back to the men on the ground.

"I'll pass the girl down to you first," he called. "Then the woman. Pete and I'll follow."

He picked Sarah up, cradling her in his arms. He reassured the softly weeping child. "Everything's all right now, bet your pretty hat on it. These men will take you off the train, then we'll give them your mom. It'll only be a minute until you're both safe and sound."

Jim lifted Sarah over the side of the coach, breathing a sigh of relief when a pair of strong arms grasped her and carried her to safety.

"Ready for the woman?" he asked, as soon as Sarah was on the ground.

"Send her down," the brakeman said.

Cautiously, Jim slid Sarah's mother over the edge of the coach, lowering her to the men waiting below. A moment later, she lay a safe distance from the burning car, with Sarah at her side.

"You're next, Pete," Jim ordered. "I'll catch up to you in a minute."

"I'll buy the drinks," Pete grinned. He painfully twisted around to drop off the car. The awaiting men below grunted with the effort as they took hold of the muscular cowboy and lowered him gently to the ground.

"We're ready for you, mister," the brakeman called.

"Comin' right down," Jim replied. He gripped the edge of the coach and lowered himself over the side. Two pairs of strong hands broke his fall as he dropped.

Jim gasped at the pain in his side. "Appreciate your help," he said. He rolled onto his stomach and choked up thick, black phlegm. Revived somewhat by the cool night air, he pushed himself upright. The devastation that met his eyes stunned him.

Leaping flames pierced the darkness and illuminated the grim scene with an eerie, flickering light which revealed the train's locomotive toppled onto its side, steam still escaping from its ruptured boiler. Behind the tender, the express car was still on the tracks, but the next two coaches lay on their sides and ablaze. The last coach was still upright, but behind it, the cattle car was derailed, and Sam whinnied shrilly for release. Injured passengers lay where they'd been pulled from the wreckage, some lying silently, others moaning with pain. Jim staggered over to Pete, Sarah, and her mother.

"Help these folks the best ya can, Pete," Jim said. I'll get back quick as I can."

"I'd go with you if I could," Pete said. He grimaced as he once again tried his broken leg. "Anyway, I'll keep an eye on the girl and her mom."

He gave Sarah a reassuring smile.

"Appreciate that," Jim said. He hurried to join the rescue efforts, shouting to Sam as he did.

"I'll be with you in a bit, Sam! I'll have you outta there right quick."

The flames still had to eat through the upright passenger car before they reached the cattle car, so the big paint would be safer confined than loose, at least for the moment.

"Hey, cowboy, give me a hand!" someone

shouted, as Jim trotted toward the overturned locomotive. He turned to see a fat drummer pulling an unconscious soldier from the first coach. Jim turned to help the sweating drummer pull his burden to safety. As they placed the soldier on the ground the conductor, Mike Hardy, rushed up.

"Mister, I've been lookin' all over for you," Hardy shouted at Jim. "I need you to get that horse of yours out of the cattle car. Now!"

"What d'ya mean?" Jim replied, puzzled. "How about gettin' the rest of the passengers out first?"

"Because in a few minutes there could be a lot more dead folks," Hardy snapped. "The eastbound local is due through here anytime now. It's probably already passed through Breckenridge, so it won't stop again until Mineral Wells. With the depth of that cut in front of us, and a blind curve just ahead, the crew won't see this wreck until it's too late. They'll smash right into us, head on. The only chance we've got is for you to take your horse, ride up the tracks a mile or so, and flag down that train. Here's a stop lamp."

Hardy shoved a red-globed lantern into Jim's hand.

"You'd better get movin'. There's no time to waste."

"On my way," Jim replied. He turned and ran for the cattle car, swinging the lantern as he went.

• • •

The fire had eaten its way toward the cattle car far more rapidly than Jim had expected. Sam whinnied frantically for release from what was now his prison.

Jim spoke calmly to reassure his paint.

"I'll have you outta there in a jiffy, Sam, bet a hat on it."

He muttered in frustration when he attempted to slide the door open. The derailment had bent the car's frame, jamming the latch shut. Desperately, Jim looked around for something, anything he could use to bust open that door. He spotted a length of thick metal torn from one of the cars. He trotted over and grabbed the piece, then shoved it behind the door latch as a makeshift lever. Jim's muscles bulged as he pulled back on the bar with all the strength he could muster. With a screech of yielding metal, the door scraped back a few inches. Jim put his shoulder to the door, pushed it all the way open, and jumped into the car.

Sam nuzzled his shoulder and nickered. He dropped his nose to Jim's hip pocket, begging for a peppermint.

"There's no time for that," Jim told the gelding. "We've got to get you out of here."

He untied the paint, then retrieved his saddle, bridle, and Winchester from the corner. He slid the rifle into its scabbard, tossed the blanket over

Sam's back, set the saddle in place, and quickly tightened the cinch.

"You're gonna have to jump, Sam," he said, leading him to the door. Sam pulled back, snorting.

"You've got no choice. Now jump!" he ordered.

Jim leapt out of the car, pulling Sam's lead. With a final squeal of protest, Sam followed his rider. As his back hooves cleared the edge of the door, the hay scattered on the floor burst into flame.

Jim set the lantern on the ground and spoke to the horse in a gentle, soothing tone of voice.

"We've gotta hurry, or there'll be a lot more dead folks around here."

He made sure the cinch was tight, then slipped the bridle's bit into Sam's mouth and the headstall over his ears. He retrieved the lantern, climbed into the saddle, and sent Sam forward at a cautious jogtrot.

As they came alongside the express car, the bodies of the messengers, one draped over the doorsill, the other sprawled on the ground, were luridly illuminated by the blaze.

"Whoa up a minute, Sam," Jim ordered. He tugged on the reins, pulling the horse to a halt. Jim got down, swiftly examined the bodies, then remounted and turned Sam back along the wreckage, until he located Mike Hardy. The conductor was bandaging an injured boy's arm.

"What're you still doin' here?" Hardy demanded, when he saw Jim. "I told you, the local's due anytime now."

"Don't worry about that," Jim retorted. "Sam'll get me out ahead in time to stop that train. But until I get back, nobody's to touch anything in the express car."

"Why?" Hardy asked.

"This train was wrecked on purpose," Jim replied. "Both of the messengers are dead . . . shot to death."

"You can't be serious," Hardy said.

"I'm dead serious," Jim answered. "And I meant exactly what I said. No one goes near that car until I get back."

"Who the devil do you think you are, giving me orders?" Hardy protested. "You don't have any authority on this railroad."

"This gives me the authority," Jim said. He dug into his vest pocket, came up with his badge, and pinned it to his vest. "I'm a Texas Ranger."

"A Ranger!" Hardy stared at the badge in surprise, then nodded. "I'll see to it," he said.

Jim whirled Sam on his heels and disappeared into the night.

CHAPTER THREE

"We'll have to be real careful, Sam. You make one mistake and it'll be all over for both of us," Jim warned his horse. They worked their way past the shattered barrier of boulders and downed trees which had doomed the El Paso Limited, then traced a path through the pitch-black canyon which the railroad had cut even deeper to level the trackbed and lessen the grade. The walls of the canyon through which the tracks snaked loomed ominously overhead, blotting out all but the slightest illumination from the stars. He guided Sam only lightly with the reins, for the most part giving the horse his head, allowing the sure-footed gelding to pick his way over the rough gravel ballast and thick wooden ties of the roadbed. If the big paint made one misstep, and put a hoof into a hole or caught a foot in the space between a tie and rail, he could easily snap a leg. In the darkness, it was far better to rely on Sam's eyesight and instincts.

"Easy, pard," Jim cautioned, when Sam, in his eagerness to get away from the wrecked train, stumbled over a rough patch of roadbed. "We've still got a ways to go."

Sam snorted, tossed his head, then moved steadily onward.

After nearly a mile, the tracks finally emerged from the deep cut through the rimrock and onto a broad, level plain. Under the faint light of a setting crescent moon, the twin ribbons of steel glimmered into the distance. Far out on the plain a pinprick of light appeared, rapidly growing larger as it headed directly for the Ranger.

"Looks like we're just in time," Jim muttered, and sighed with relief. He swung out of the saddle and slapped Sam on the rump to send him trotting to safety. After fishing a lucifer from his shirt pocket, Jim opened the lantern's glass panel which allowed access to the wick, struck the match, and touched it to the wick. Once the wick caught, he closed the chimney and stepped into the middle of the tracks, waiting anxiously.

The rails began to vibrate and hum as the local drew closer, the chuffing of the locomotive coming to Jim's ears and its plume of smoke drifting across the sky. Ignoring the pain in his ribs, Jim lifted the lantern high and swung it back and forth to signal the train to a halt.

The engine's whistle sounded a long, frantic warning as the headlight's beam swept over the man standing in the middle of the tracks. As the train thundered nearer, Jim readied himself to jump aside at the last moment. Finally, the high-pitched screeching of metal grinding on metal pierced the night when the engineer slammed on the brakes. The locomotive shuddered to a halt less than fifty feet from where Jim stood. Even before the train stopped rolling, the conductor leapt from the first coach and headed for the silhouetted figure on the tracks.

"Mister, are you plumb loco? What's the big idea?" he began, then fell silent upon seeing the battered Ranger's grim-faced visage and the silver star in silver circle badge pinned to his vest glittering in the lantern's light.

The engineer climbed from his cab and joined the conductor. "Pat, what in blue blazes is goin' on?" he asked. Jim broke in before the trainman could respond.

"The El Paso Limited's been wrecked, just about two miles back," he explained. "I had to stop your train before you smashed into the barrier someone used to derail it."

"What's that? The El Paso Limited's wrecked?" the conductor echoed, only to be interrupted by Jim once again.

"Get those people back on the train," Jim ordered, as he spotted curious passengers alighting from the cars. "I need you to run this thing slowly up to the wreck. There's a lot of injured folks who need to get to a doctor as quick as possible. You're gonna load the people from the Limited onto this train and haul 'em to Breckenridge."

"Yes sir, Ranger," the conductor replied. He

turned to shout an order to a crewman. "Sal, get everyone back on board."

He turned to the engineer.

"Jack, have Sully get steam back up, and we'll get rollin'," he ordered, then returned his attention to Jim.

"What about you, Ranger? You need a ride?"

"Nope," Jim replied. "I've got my horse, right over there." He waved a hand in Sam's direction. The paint was cropping grass alongside the tracks, patiently awaiting his rider.

"I'll ride back. Since you'll be movin' slow, I'll make just as good time ridin' him as I would ridin' the cars. Besides, I doubt you're haulin' a cattle car, and I sure ain't leavin' Sam behind. I'll meet you back at the wreck."

"All right, Ranger, and thanks," the conductor answered. "You saved some lives tonight."

The first light of dawn was just gilding the eastern horizon pink and gold when Jim and his horse returned to the site of the derailment. The eastbound local had reached the wrecked express only moments before. Its passengers and crew had already alighted from the train to assist the injured.

The rising sun, sending fingers of light to penetrate the depths of the canyon, revealed the full extent of the devastation. After chewing its way through all but half of the last coach, the fire had burned itself out, leaving mounds of twisted, blackened rubble. Smoke still rose from the debris, fouling the cool morning air. Injured passengers were scattered about, lying where they'd been pulled from the wreckage, and tended to by the less gravely wounded. Several still, blanket-covered forms were mute testimony that the men who had wrecked the El Paso Limited had done their work only too well.

Dismounting and leading Sam, Jim headed for where he recalled leaving Pete, Sarah, and Sarah's mother, but they were no longer there. His heart pounded as he anxiously scanned the vicinity for sign of them.

"Hey, Jim, over here!" Pete called.

Jim breathed a sigh of relief. He hurried to where Pete lay with a rude splint bound to his broken leg. Pete was smiling at the woman sitting beside him. She had a look of deep concern on her face as she gazed at him. A clean, white strip from a petticoat was wrapped around her head as a makeshift bandage, which covered her forehead.

"Jim, I'd like you to meet Mrs. Lottie Parker," Pete introduced her. "You already know her daughter, of course. Miz Parker, this is the *hombre* I told you about."

Pete glanced at the badge pinned to Jim's vest.

"You're a Ranger, huh? Any truth to the story goin' around that this train was deliberately wrecked?"

"You've got me pegged," Jim admitted. "Far as the wreck, it seems that way. I've still got to do more checking."

Turning to Lottie Parker, he lifted two fingers to the brim of his Stetson, and nodded a polite greeting.

"Ma'am", Jim said, smiling. "I'm sure glad to see you've come around. We were all really worried about you."

"Thanks to you, Mister . . . I'm sorry, Mr. Cummings didn't tell me your last name," she replied.

"That's because he doesn't know it," Jim explained. "It's Blawcyzk. That's BLUH-zhick," he repeated, knowing most folks didn't catch his surname the first time. "Easier to just call me Jim."

"And don't forget, I told you to call me Pete, not Mr. Cummings," the cowboy broke in.

"Fine, as long as you both call me Lottie." She turned back to Jim. "Pete told me what you did. I don't know how I can ever thank you. My husband died last year, and I couldn't bear the thought of Sarah being left alone."

"No thanks necessary," Jim replied, watching Sam, who was gently nuzzling Sarah. "Besides, Pete deserves at least as much credit as I do, mebbe more. I couldn't have gotten you and Sarah out of that car without his help."

Sarah laughed when Sam nuzzled her more insistently.

"How are you feeling, Sarah?" Jim asked. "Didn't I promise you that your mom would be just fine?"

"Yes," Sarah answered shyly. Then she burst into giggles when Sam pressed his velvety nose even harder against her cheek.

"Your horse's whiskers tickle."

"Then you must be a very special young lady," Jim said. "Sam doesn't take to very many folks."

"Jim," Lottie continued. "You're much too modest. I know you saved all of our lives, and I'll be forever grateful."

"Nothing anyone else wouldn't have done," Jim demurred, his face coloring with embarrassment at her praise. "Now, I've got to see if I can help any of the others. After that, I've got to look over the express car. Is there anything either of you need before I go?"

"Don't worry about Mr. Cummings, I mean, Pete," Lottie replied. "I'll look after him."

"And I'll look after both Lottie and Sarah," Pete added.

"That's just fine. Sarah, you keep an eye on your mom and Pete for me, all right? I'll be back as quick as I can."

39

"Sure, Ranger Jim," Sarah replied. She patted Sam's neck.

"All right, then," Jim answered. "C'mon, Sam." He swung into the saddle.

As he headed for the express car, a slight smile played across Jim's face. Judging from the way Pete and Lottie had been looking at each other, at least one good thing might well have come from the wrecking of the El Paso Limited.

Mike Hardy intercepted Jim just before he reached the express car.

"Ranger, I've been lookin' all over for you," the conductor said. "It seems like you were right about someone wreckin' this train on purpose. Chip Danvers wants to talk with you."

"Danvers? You mean the engineer?" Jim said. From what he'd seen of the crushed remains of the locomotive, it seemed impossible that anyone in its cab could have survived.

"We managed to pull him out of the smashed cab, but he's in bad shape," Hardy explained. "He's not gonna last, so we'd better hurry. He's right over there."

Hardy quickened his pace as he indicated where the gravely injured Danvers lay, under some stunted redberry junipers.

Mike Jones, the brakeman, was tending to the dying engineer. He looked up and shook his head when Hardy and Jim approached.

"Chip's just about gone," he whispered to Hardy, then glanced at Jim. "He's been tryin' to hang on until you returned, Ranger. Dunno if he can still talk, or not."

To Jim's surprise, a bullet hole was evident, high in Danvers' chest. When he hunkered alongside the horribly crushed engineer, Danvers' eyes flickered open.

"You're . . . a . . . Ranger," he stammered, struggling to speak. "Guess we know now . . . why we had to . . . hold this train."

"Take it easy," Jim urged. "You have somethin' to tell me?"

"Yeah . . . yeah." Danvers' voice was barely a whisper. "Mike told me you said this train was wrecked on purpose. You're right, Ranger." Danvers paused, gasping for breath. "Saw . . . four men with rifles . . . on the slide blockin' the track. Thought I was gonna be able to . . . stop the train . . . in time until . . . one of 'em . . . plugged me. Shot me right off the brake . . . lever."

Danvers' eyes closed, and his voice faded.

"Poor Suggs. He didn't have . . . a chance," he quavered.

Jim looked at Hardy.

"Suggs?" he questioned.

"Leo Suggs, the fireman. We couldn't pull him out of the cab. He was already dead when we got to him. He was pinned against the fire jacket and scalded to death by the steam."

41

Hardy shivered at the thought.

Danvers' eyes opened one final time. They were glazed with pain.

"Ranger . . ."

"I'm right here, Chip."

"All I'm askin' is you get the skunks who did this."

"You've got my word on it," Jim said, and his words were not just assurance to the dying man. "I'll find 'em. You can bet a hat on it."

"Good. Good." Danvers sighed deeply, then his body shuddered and went slack.

Jim pushed back to his feet, grim determination in his eyes, which now glittered coldly, like chips of blue ice.

"Did anybody go near that express car yet?" Jim's eyes speared Hardy.

Hardy took an involuntary step back. "No, sir, Ranger. I made certain of that."

"Good. Come with me while I check it," Jim ordered. Once again, he headed for the express car, leading Sam with Hardy trailing behind.

"How many dead?" Jim asked.

"Seven passengers so far, plus Danvers and Suggs. Then, there's Bill Grady and Mel Logan, the messengers. We haven't yet finished searching the wreckage, of course, so there may be more. I can't figure what kind of men'd pull a stunt like this, hurtin' a bunch of innocent folks, especially women and kids."

"When I catch up to 'em, I'll be sure to ask 'em for you," Jim replied. "Before the court hangs 'em."

When they reached the express car, Jim rolled the dead messenger lying on the ground onto his back.

"That's Mel Logan," Hardy muttered, while Jim studied the bullet hole square in the center of the man's chest.

"Never knew what hit him," Jim observed. He walked over to the car's ajar door, then lowered the body of the other messenger from the car.

"They gut-shot this one. Looks like one slug went clean through and hit his spine," he noted. Bill Grady had taken two bullets through his stomach. Jim turned back to Hardy.

"What were you carryin' on this run?" he asked.

"Besides the usual stuff, United States Mail, merchandise, luggage, we have thirty thousand dollars in new double eagles bound for the bank in Abilene."

"Better make that *had* thirty thousand," Jim replied. He pulled himself into the express car. "The safe's been busted open and cleaned out." He quickly looked over the jumbled contents of the blood-splattered car. "Hard to tell the way they ransacked this car, but it doesn't look like they bothered to take anything else."

Hardy exploded with an oath.

"Looks like they got clean away with it, too.

Well, with any luck someone'll blast those coyotes clean to Hades."

"They haven't gotten away quite yet," Jim answered. He climbed out of the car and whistled Sam over. Once the paint reached his side, he stood patiently, waiting while Jim dug in his saddlebags for a scrap of paper and stub of pencil.

"What're you meanin' to do?" Hardy asked.

"Go after 'em," Jim said, "What else?"

"You can't. They've got almost a whole night's start, and besides, you're hurt," Hardy protested. "Plus, I'll bet you haven't had anything to eat or drink."

"Don't matter," Jim answered. "They'll have to travel slow, with their horses weighted down by that gold. I'm gonna track 'em down. I've got some jerky in my saddlebags, and I'll find a waterhole. These bruises look a lot worse'n they feel. I do need you to do one thing for me, however."

Jim placed the paper on his saddle and quickly scrawled, *El Paso train wrecked and robbed. On trail of bandits. Will wire soon as possible. JB.*

Once finished, he handed the scrap to Hardy, who glanced it over.

"That's it?" Hardy asked.

"That's it," Jim confirmed. "Send that message to Captain Hank Trumbull at Ranger Headquarters in Austin the minute you reach Breckenridge."

"Sure will, Ranger." Hardy sized up the battered, exhausted lawman. "You positive about goin' after those *hombres*?

"Absolutely," Jim replied. He tightened his cinch and swung into the saddle. He turned Sam toward the shattered slide, the earth, rocks and trees the robbers had used to barricade the tracks.

"Well, then, good luck," Hardy offered.

"Appreciate that," Jim said. He heeled Sam into a slow jogtrot.

CHAPTER FOUR

Jim dismounted once he reached the remains of the barricade which had destroyed the El Paso Limited. He dropped to his knees to study more closely the bootprints which indicated where four men had hidden in a dense patch of cedars and scrub brush, waiting to strike the instant the train was derailed.

"They headed off this way, Sam," he told his horse, remounting. Putting Sam into an easy walk, he followed the footprints to a slot in the canyon's wall, where the outlaws' horses had been hidden. Jim's gaze lifted to a narrow path, which snaked its way up the wall of the canyon.

"That's the only way outta here, pard, which means they sure didn't double back. Should be easy enough to trail 'em for a while, anyway."

Jim sighed with resignation as he heeled Sam into a faster walk, then a trot.

With only one trail out of the canyon, Jim was able to make good time for quite some distance, even allowing his horse to lope in some of the wider sections of the trail. A few hundred yards before reaching the rim, however, the trail became barely wide enough for Sam to plant all four feet. Jim's right stirrup scraped a solid red-rock wall, impossible to climb, and to the left was a sheer drop of two hundred feet or more.

"Don't you slip, horse, or there won't be enough left of us to pick up with a spoon," Jim said. "Just take it slow and real careful-like." He loosened the reins even more, allowing Sam to pick his way. He breathed a sigh of relief when the trail widened as they neared the top.

At the lip of the canyon, the hoofprints of the outlaws' horses led out of the defile and onto a fairly level plateau, dotted with cedars and post oaks.

"They're still not tryin' to cover their tracks, Sam," Jim said, as he pushed his horse into a hard gallop. "Must've figured they made a clean getaway, or else that no one'd get on their trail right quick. Reckon that means we don't have to worry about anyone tryin' to ambush us, at least for a while."

He let Sam run until the trail ducked back into another canyon.

The trail the fugitives were taking wound through the low, but rugged, Palo Pinto Mountains. As the path climbed higher into the hills the terrain became more rocky and broken, the hoofprints harder to follow. As the sun passed its zenith, the long ordeal began to wear on man and mount. Jim's head throbbed from the blow to his skull he'd suffered during the derailment, and the pain in his side, which had settled to a dull ache, was once again shooting through his ribs. The sharp, stabbing pain more than once had him doubled over in the saddle. Except for some bites of jerky for Jim and a few snatches of bunch grass Sam had been allowed during brief moments of rest, neither had eaten since leaving Dallas. Sam's pace slowed to a plodding walk.

"Gotta find some water, and pretty quick, too," Jim muttered, when his belly growled yet again. "Neither one of us can go much further without it."

He lifted the reins and clucked encouragingly to his tired horse.

Once again, the hoofprints of the outlaws' horses led into another of a seemingly interminable series of canyons.

"At least we're gainin' on 'em some, horse," Jim assured Sam. "They're not in any hurry."

Sam nickered a soft response, then lifted his head. His nostrils flared as he keened the air. The big gelding broke into an eager trot as he scented water.

"Easy there, bud," Jim warned, when Sam started to break into a lope. "We've gotta scout the situation first, just in case our friends up ahead decided to take a rest. Wouldn't do to just ride in on 'em, four to one is not good odds, y'know." Jim chuckled. "Despite what people say about one Ranger bein' able to handle a whole passel of outlaws all by himself."

Jim pulled his paint back to a reluctant walk, then a short distance on reined him to a halt. He looped his reins over the saddlehorn and dismounted, leaving Sam hidden in a small grove of junipers.

"You wait right here," he ordered, giving the gelding a peppermint. "And keep quiet."

Sam would wait until his rider whistled him up. Jim slid his rifle from its saddle boot, then, with a final pat to his horse's nose, slipped silently up the trail.

"Looks like they rode on," Jim muttered a few minutes later. To his disappointment, there was no sign of his quarry. Evidently, they had stopped just long enough to have a quick drink, water their horses, and fill their canteens, then ridden on. Jim hurried back to where Sam was waiting, then led him to a small *cienega*, which was fed by water seeping from the base of an eroding red rock wall.

After watering Sam sparingly, Jim pulled off his Stetson and bandanna. He drank his fill, then ducked his head into the spring. The soothing water cooled his face's sun-parched skin. Jim next soaked his bandanna, running the cloth over his neck and shoulders.

"I'm gonna give you a half-hour's rest," he told Sam, when the horse nuzzled his chest. "Then we're gonna push on, and see if we can catch up with these jaspers before nightfall."

Sam fell to cropping at the lush grass surrounding the spring. Jim stretched out on the ground, pulled his Stetson over his eyes, and was instantly asleep.

In less than an hour, Jim woke and hit the trail once again. Many years and long miles of chasing outlaws had toughened him so, despite his injuries, he was greatly refreshed by the alltoo-brief respite. Sam, having drunk and eaten, was also ready to travel again.

"Doggoned if they ain't headin' back towards Breckenridge," Jim muttered, when he realized the trail first headed north, then curved steadily westward as it wound deeper into the hills.

Two hours after leaving the waterhole, Jim pulled Sam to a halt. He lifted his Stetson from his head. He wiped moisture from its band, then scratched his sweat-soaked thatch of blonde hair in puzzlement.

"Looks like they split up here, Sam," he said. "Wonder what the devil that's all about?"

Two sets of hoofprints headed left, down a steep side trail and into a sandy arroyo, while the others continued straight ahead. Jim dismounted, to hunker on his heels and study the tracks carefully. As was his habit, he discussed the situation with his patient horse.

"Which ones do you think we should follow, Sam?"

Sam's response was a disgusted snort. He shook his head.

"Guess you're right," Jim chuckled. "It doesn't hardly matter which ones we pick."

He pulled his canteen from the saddlehorn, poured some water into his hat and gave Sam a short drink, then allowed himself a quick pull on the canteen. Swinging back into the saddle, he heeled Sam into a walk, following the hoofprints that led straight ahead.

"I reckon those prints in that sand'll last longer, unless we get a cloudburst, pard," he said to Sam. "I figure we can try and catch up with this pair first, then double back and track down the others if need be. It looks like we might only be a coupl'a hours behind 'em." Fighting his weariness, Jim pushed on.

Three hours later, just before sunset, Jim pushed Sam up a rise. The tracks of the outlaws' horses were now fairly fresh. Without warning, Sam halted, his ears pricked forward and nostrils flaring as he sniffed the air.

"What's out there, pal?" Jim asked, straining to hear or see whatever had alerted his horse.

"Smoke!" he exclaimed when the unmistakable scent of a wood fire drifted to his nose. "Better leave you here, while I have a looksee."

Jim slid out of the saddle and led Sam into the shelter of a nest of concealing boulders.

"You wait here," he ordered. "I'll be right back."

Working as silently as possible, he stalked carefully to just below the rise's summit, then dropped to his belly to crawl the last hundred feet.

"Gotcha," Jim whispered in satisfaction, as he overlooked a small, grassy valley. In the center of the valley stood a small, rundown shack, with smoke curling lazily from its chimney. Two horses, a bay and a blue roan, stood hipshot in a small enclosure.

Shouldn't be all that difficult to corral these two renegades, Jim thought, while he studied the terrain. Clumps of mesquite and large prickly pear, plus scattered cedars and live oak, provided decent cover to within a few feet of the cabin. He lifted his Colt from its holster, slipped a cartridge into the empty cylinder under the hammer, then slid the gun back into place. Cautiously, he worked his way down the slope, slipping through the brush almost as silently as a Comanche.

"Hope these *hombres* aren't expectin' any company," Jim murmured once he reached the last of his cover, a scraggly mesquite bush. He pulled his pistol from its holster, sprinted across the clearing, and burst through the shack's door, his Colt leveled for action.

"Texas Ranger! You're under arrest," Jim shouted at the two men who sat at a rude plank table in the middle of the room. Their eyes were wide with disbelief as they stared at the badge on Jim's chest, and the Colt in his hand.

"Stand up, real slow and easy, and keep those hands where I can see them," he ordered.

"Sure, sure Ranger," said one of the men. The swarthy dark-haired man, his dark eyes muddy, started to rise, then, with a snarling curse, he leapt up, toppling the table and yanking at his six-gun. Jim triggered his pistol. The bullet plowed into the swarthy outlaw's chest and dropped him to the floor, motionless.

A bullet from the second renegade's gun whined over Jim's right shoulder. Jim shifted his pistol and fired twice. Both slugs tore into the outlaw's belly, just above his belt buckle, and he triggered his second shot harmlessly into the ceiling. The sallow-faced killer grabbed desperately at his middle and staggered back against the wall. With a groan, he jackknifed, then pitched onto his face. Jim pulled the gun from his hand, tossed it into the corner, and rolled him onto his back. The amount of blood spreading over his shirtfront indicated at least one of Jim's bullets had severed a major artery or vein. The outlaw moaned once, let out a deep sigh, and breathed his last.

"Blast it!" Jim checked the pair but recognized neither. "I wanted to take these jaspers alive."

He reloaded his Colt and slid it back into its holster. A quick search of the bodies provided no clues to their identities. Stepping to the door, Jim whistled shrilly, and an answering whinny drifted over the hill. Soon Sam trotted into sight, then galloped down the ridge and up to where Jim stood waiting. Jim glanced at the stove in the corner of the cabin. His mouth watered at the tantalizing aromas of frying bacon, boiling coffee, and rising biscuits, the meal those two renegades would never get to eat.

"Reckon we eat good tonight, anyway, Sam," Jim said, scratching the paint's ears. "My supper's cookin', and I'd imagine I'll find you some oats and hay around here somewhere."

Sam nickered softly, nuzzled Jim's shoulder, then dropped his nose to Jim's hip pocket, begging for a peppermint.

"All right, beggar," Jim chuckled. He dug in his pocket, came up with a candy, and gave it to Sam, who crunched down happily on the treat.

Gotta figure out what in blue blazes to do with these hombres, Jim thought. He stripped the gear from his horse, then turned him into the corral along with the outlaws' mounts. He'd decided, with night coming on, and he and his horse both badly in need of rest, to spend the night in the shack. Besides, he had a hunch the dead men's partners would show up sometime before morning.

There was a lean-to at the back of the corral, where saddle gear and blankets were stored. Jim dragged the dead men behind the shed, speaking softly to the outlaws' alarmed, snorting horses as he went. He covered the bodies with some old horse blankets, scattered hay over them to further conceal them, then brushed out the drag marks as best he could.

"I can't leave you out here, in case their pards show up," he said to Sam, who was gratefully munching hay. "There's nowhere to hide you but inside the shack. You'll get your oats there." He paused and chuckled. "C'mon, but you'd better not snore, horse."

After filling a coffee can with oats from a bin in the lean-to and grabbing a flake of hay, Jim tossed his gear onto Sam's back once again, then led the gelding back to the cabin, through the door and into a corner of the room. Jim lifted his saddle from his paint's back and dropped it to the floor. Sam buried his muzzle in Jim's belly, causing him to grunt, then nosed Jim's hip pocket, looking for the peppermint he always received at the end of the day. With a laugh, Jim produced the treat, which Sam happily took. Once he'd poured out the grain and tossed the hay into a corner of the cramped, dirty room, Jim righted the upset table, found a tin plate and mug, and settled to his own supper, eagerly consuming fifteen slices of bacon and half a dozen biscuits, washing those down with three mugs of thick, black coffee. As the sun set, Jim took the stub of a candle stuck in the mouth of a bitters jar down from the shack's only shelf, set it on the table, and lit it.

"Now, let's see where these two might've hidden their loot," he said, glancing around the cabin's single room. His search didn't take long. In a matter of minutes he discovered two pairs of saddlebags, carelessly hidden under the thin mattress on one of the bunks. Jim nodded in satisfaction after examining the contents.

"Got a good chunk of the money here, Sam," he said. "And with any luck, I'll get the rest when I catch up to their pardners."

As exhaustion overtook him, Jim slid the gold-laden saddlebags back under the bunk, blew out the candle, then settled back on the straw-filled mattress, still fully-dressed, secure in the knowledge that Sam would alert him to any danger. He yawned and stretched, and before he could even finish his evening prayers, Jim was sound asleep.

It was full dark when a soft nicker from Sam jerked Jim out of his sleep. In the dim moonlight from the window, Jim could see his horse, who was standing alertly in the corner, his ears pricked sharply forward. The soft clopping of horses' hooves cut through the usual sounds of the crickets, cicadas, and other night creatures.

"Shh. Quiet, Sam," Jim warned. He rose

quietly from the bunk and slid his Colt from its holster, then took a position opposite the door, standing with six-gun leveled. He heard the riders dismount and turn their horses into the corral.

"Those lazy sons must be sleepin' real sound, Monte." The man half-laughed. "They'd better have our supper warmin' on the stove."

"I'd rather have some whiskey, Sloan." The second speaker sounded tired. "Reckon that'll have to keep until we reach town, though."

Jim tensed as their footsteps reached the shack. The door crashed open.

"Martinez, Houlihan," one of the pair called out. "Wake up, you lazy bums. You'd . . ."

He stopped in shock, staring wide-eyed at the tall figure against the wall.

"Your pardners won't be wakin' up, leastwise not in this world," Jim snapped. "Neither will you, unless you shuck those guns right now. You can bet a hat on it. Texas Ranger. You're under arrest, boys."

One of the men edged his hand toward the gun on his hip. "Uh-uh, I wouldn't try that," Jim said, "unless you want your bellybutton to meet up with your backbone. Just unbuckle your gunbelts, slow and easy, and let 'em drop."

Muttering curses, but knowing they didn't have a chance against that menacing Colt in the lawman's left hand, the men complied, carefully unhitching their gunbelts and dropping them slowly to the floor. Their eyes glittered malevolently and their faces twisted into scowls as they glared at Jim.

"That's just fine, now kick the hardware over here," Jim ordered.

The outlaws complied.

"Now drop those saddlebags."

With a shrug of resignation, both men obeyed, the hand-tooled *alforjas* hitting the rough floor of the shack with a heavy, metallic clunk.

"Now, sit down, you." Jim waggled his six-gun for emphasis. He lifted a lariat from a peg. Once the bearded outlaw had settled into a chair, Jim cut the rope, and tossed half at the man's feet. "You Monte? Or Sloan?"

"Sloan," said the man on the chair.

"You, Monte," he ordered, looking at the outlaw still standing. "Tie your pard up. Make sure the knots are good and tight."

Cursing under his breath, Monte obeyed Jim's orders. He tied Sloan's arms behind the rickety chair, then his ankles to its legs.

"Now you sit down, Monte," Jim ordered.

Jim slid his Peacemaker back into its holster and knelt to the task of tying Monte to the remaining chair.

While Jim worked at the rope, Sloan pushed himself upward, toppling the chair and diving across the plank floor to slam into Jim's back.

"Get his gun, Monte!" Sloan yelled, as Jim

thrashed spasmodically on the floor, helpless against the agony shooting through his spine. Monte grabbed Jim's gun from its holster and aimed it at his belly.

"Now let's see who's gonna get himself gut-shot, Ranger," he snarled, as he thumbed back the hammer. Jim's stomach muscles tensed in anticipation of hot lead tearing into his belly and ripping through his guts. Then Sam, trumpeting his fury, smashed into Monte just as he pulled the trigger. The heavy .45 slug he'd meant for Jim's belly instead ricocheted off the rusted sheet-metal stove to tear through Sloan's throat. The bearded outlaw, still tied, uttered a choked gurgle as life-blood drained from his severed jugular.

Sam drove into Monte again, knocking him to his knees. The Colt went spinning to the floor and the outlaw scrambled for it. Jim fought the pain that half-paralyzed his back and side and managed to pull his knife from its sheath. He threw it straight at Monte's chest. The Bowie's heavy blade buried itself to the hilt in Monte's chest, piercing his heart. As blood crimsoned his shirtfront, Monte thumb-cocked the six-gun and squeezed the trigger one last time. This bullet burned a path along Jim's right ribs. Monte collapsed, face down, dead.

Gasping, pulling air into his tortured lungs, Jim got shakily to his feet. He leaned against Sam for support.

"Thanks, Sam," he said. "Reckon I owe you my life . . . again."

The big gelding nuzzled Jim's chest and whickered softly.

"Yeah, I know," Jim said, smiling. He dug into his hip pocket, came up with a peppermint, and slipped it to Sam. "Don't matter what happens to me, long as you get your peppermints. Well, let's see what we can do about these two *hombres*."

Jim retrieved his gun, reloaded it, and placed it back in its holster. He pulled his knife from Monte's chest, wiped it clean on the outlaw's shirt, and used the Bowie to cut the ropes that held Sloan to the chair. After taking a moment to catch his breath again, he checked the bodies. As with the other two men, their clothing yielded no clues as to their identities or backgrounds. Too tired and hurt to pull the bodies behind the lean-to, he merely dragged them out of the shack, stumbled back in and closed the door. He picked up their saddlebags and placed them alongside the others under the bunk.

"Reckon we won't have to worry about anyone else droppin' in for a visit tonight, Sam," Jim observed, as he managed to shrug out of his shirt. He pulled his medical kit from his saddlebags, then proceeded to clean, dress, and bandage the bullet slash along his ribs.

Jim's head still throbbed. Pain stabbed at his side as he pulled off his boots and gingerly lay back onto the bunk. His left side sported a huge purple bruise where the beam had smashed into him when the El Paso Limited derailed. His right side stung where the bullet slashed it, and his back muscles still spasmed once in a while where Sloan had driven the edge of his chair into them. Nonetheless, with a feeling of grim satisfaction he drifted off into a sound, dreamless sleep. He'd tracked down the men who'd wrecked and robbed the El Paso Limited, and recovered the money. He only regretted that he'd been forced to kill the outlaws instead of being able to bring them in to face the court's justice.

CHAPTER FIVE

As always, Jim was up before the sun. When he rolled out of the bunk, his ribs were still stiff and sore, but the worst of the pain was gone, and the throbbing in his head had subsided to a dull ache. While he sat on the edge of the bunk, pulling on his boots, Sam came up to him. He buried his muzzle in Jim's middle and whickered like he was asking a question.

"Yeah, you're right, we've gotta get movin'," Jim said, giving Sam's ears a friendly tweak. "Soon's I rustle up some grub and load those *hombres* on their horses, we'll be on our way. With luck, we'll make town well before nightfall."

He stood up, pulled on his shirt, and jammed his Stetson on his head.

"There, I'm set, pal. Meantime, let's see if I can come up with some more grain for you. Got to be a bait of it around here somewhere."

When Sam nickered as if in agreement, Jim added, chuckling, "Besides, a horse don't belong in a cabin anyhow. Good thing you were, though. Saved me from a point-blank bullet through my guts."

Sam snorted as if disgusted when Jim led him

back outside and he saw the bodies of Monte and Sloan.

"Easy, bud," he chided, when Sam pinned back his ears and bared his teeth, plunging his head toward Monte's remains. "You took care of him good and proper last night. Time to fill your belly. We've got to put quite a few miles behind us today."

He led Sam into the corral, where a chestnut mare and blaze-faced sorrel gelding had joined the bay and blue roan. He discovered another grain bin, this one half-full, just under the lean-to's roof, partially hidden by an old tarp. He filled a bucket with oats and poured out a good measure for each animal, then forked hay into the corral from a pile outside. He filled two buckets with water and placed these inside the corral. The horses fed, he went behind the lean-to to relieve himself. After that he quickly washed up in the small creek which ran past the cabin, then turned his attention to his own meal. He made a fresh pot of coffee, then downed a quick breakfast of leftover bacon and beans. Despite his haste, Jim took the dishes to the creek and washed them, then returned them to their place on the shelf. That chore completed, he closed the cabin door and dragged the bodies of Monte and Sloan to the corral. He saddled the outlaws' mounts, tossed the saddlebags over their backs and fastened those in place, tied the horses to the fence, then threw his gear on Sam. He pulled two more musty blankets from the shed, wrapped Monte's and Sloan's bodies, then retrieved the bodies of Martinez and Houlihan, tying the blankets around them.

Speaking softly, Jim's calm voice soothed the outlaws' nervously dancing horses. Jim had to struggle against the pain of his cracked ribs and bad back, but managed to drape the rigor-mortis stiffened dead men belly-down over their saddles. He lashed them securely in place. He hitched the four horses together, then tied the lead animal's rope to his saddle horn, then swung onto Sam's back.

"Let's get goin', pard," he ordered the paint, nudging his spurless bootheels into Sam's ribs, to push him into a fast walk. "It's about twenty miles to Breckenridge, if I'm calculatin' right. Reckon we should make town just about mid-afternoon."

As Jim worked his way westward, the rugged canyons and slopes of the Palo Pintos gradually descended to the rolling plains of north-central Texas. Trees and scrub brush thinned out, the land now given more to tough buffalo, grama, and bunch grasses, interspersed with clumps of prickly pear and yucca. Lines of brush and cottonwoods marked the occasional creek. At mid-morning, Jim stopped at a nameless tributary of the Brazos River. Picketing the outlaws' horses and turning Sam loose, he allowed the mounts to drink and graze, while he chewed on some jerky from his saddlebags, washing it down with a swallow from his canteen.

"*Rio de el Brazos de Dios*," Jim mused, gazing across the plains and up at the brilliant blue sky, which was punctuated by puffy white clouds. "River of the Arms of God. Those Spanish explorers sure got it right."

He glanced at the dead outlaws, draped over their horses.

"Too bad greedy sidewinders like those have to go and ruin a fine land like this for decent folks." He sighed deeply. "Well, mebbe someday things will change, and people'll all learn to get along. 'Course, Sam," he added with a laugh, "When that day comes, you and I'll be out of a job."

Patting Sam's shoulder, he pulled himself back into the saddle, wincing at the pain in his side.

"Let's keep movin', pal. We're not makin' as good time as I'd hoped we would."

He gathered up the other horses' lead ropes, then pushed Sam into an easy lope.

Slowed by the four horses carrying their grim burdens, Jim's journey to Breckenridge took longer than he had hoped. It was late that afternoon before the worn-out Blawcyzk, with Sam plodding wearily underneath him, rode down the dusty main street of the town. Curious townspeople who spotted the battered Ranger, marked by the silver star in silver circle badge pinned to his chest, and who led a procession of four horses carrying blanket-wrapped bodies, followed Jim as he headed for the sheriff's office. He ignored the questions shouted by a few of the bolder onlookers. After a few blocks, he reached his destination and reined Sam to a halt in front of an unpainted, rough plank building marked "Breckenridge and Stephens County Sheriff's Office and Jail."

After Jim had dismounted and was tossing Sam's reins over the hitchrail, a man of about forty, with a sheriff's star pinned to his vest, emerged from the office. He carried a shotgun, while a slight paunch pushed out his dirty brown shirt and the gunbelt around his hips. He gazed at Jim with curiosity in his washed-out gray eyes. He pushed back his back his hat on his head.

"I reckon you'd be Lieutenant . . . heck, I can't pronounce that doggone last name," he said.

"BLUH-zhick," Jim said.

"Blawcyzk," the sheriff repeated. He eyed the dead outlaws through narrowed eyes. "Looks like you've been busy. What'cha got there?"

"The *hombres* who wrecked the El Paso Limited," Jim replied, weariness in his voice. He began tying the rest of the horses to the rail. "I've got the gold they stole, too. It's in their saddlebags. I'd appreciate it if you'd tell me where to take these bodies, and where I can leave the money for safekeeping."

Then Jim paused, his blue eyes fixed on the local lawman.

"How'd you know my name, Sheriff?"

"Got a wire from Austin and I'm holdin' it for you," the sheriff answered with a shrug. "And the conductor from the train said a Ranger had gone after the men who pulled the job, and a cowboy with a busted leg mentioned you, and by the way, my handle's Dave Foster."

Foster pointed to one of the spectators. "As far as what to do with those bodies, Mort Purdy over there doubles as our undertaker, and he owns the hardware store, and I'll have a couple of men tote them dead fellers down there."

"Cecil," Foster called.

"Yeah, Sheriff," a portly, balding man in a dark suit answered.

"Ranger here's got the money from the train robbery and he'd be mighty grateful if you'd store it in your vault for the time bein'."

While the pudgy banker edged his way through the crowd, Foster explained, "Cecil Barnes is president of the bank, and he'll hold that money for you."

"That'll be fine, Sheriff," Jim said. "Thanks for your help. If you'll bring me that telegram, I'll read it on our way to the bank."

"Sure thing, Lieutenant."

Foster called to a pair of men in the crowd.

"Haskins, Reynolds. Hand me and Cecil those saddlebags and then give Mort a hand haulin' those bodies down to his place, and leave their horses at Joe's stable, until the county decides what to do with them. I imagine they'll be sold to cover the buryin' expenses, and a couple of you others help with these saddlebags, 'cause this gold's mighty heavy, and the rest of you go on about your business, 'cause the show's over."

The sheriff ducked into his office and returned a moment later with a yellow Western Union flimsy, which he handed to Jim.

Jim's eyebrows shot up as he scanned the message.

Previous orders rescinded STOP Report soon as possible to James Reasoner of the Texas and Pacific in Abilene STOP Capt H Trumbull Texas Rangers.

"Bad news, Lieutenant?" Foster asked.

"Not bad, just not what I expected," Jim answered. He folded the paper and put it in his shirt pocket, then looked up at the sheriff. "Call me Jim. It's a lot easier. Now, let's get that money in the safe, and these *hombres* on ice."

After the crowd had dispersed, and he, Foster, Barnes and two of the bystanders were headed for the bank, Jim was finally able to ask the sheriff about the passengers from the El Paso Limited.

"The local pulled in here a little before noon yesterday," Foster answered. "Doc Gorlick's made a temporary hospital down at the hotel and he's keeping the worst injured there. Luckily, most of the hurts were only bumps and bruises, plus a few broken bones."

Jim swayed slightly, and staggered with weariness. Foster looked with concern at his blood-soaked shirt.

"And mebbe you'd better see the doc yourself, Jim," he advised.

"Don't have time," Jim replied. "I've gotta finish my business here, then start out for Abilene."

He paused for a long moment, then asked the question that had been bothering him ever since the derailment.

"How many were killed in the wreck, Dave?"

"Fourteen, plus there are a couple more Doc Gorlick doesn't expect to make it."

Cecil Barnes spoke for the first time.

"It doesn't really seem like true justice, but at least the Ranger here has prevented those outlaws from ever repeating their horrible crimes."

When Jim stumbled yet again, Barnes said, "I agree with the Sheriff, Lieutenant. You really should see the doctor before you do anything else. It's over fifty miles to Abilene, and you appear completely exhausted."

"I'll be fine," Jim insisted. "Just need some hot

grub and a couple cups of coffee. Once I check on the survivors, I'll ride out."

"What about your horse?" Foster asked. "He looks done in, and you sure can't expect him to carry all this gold. It's far too heavy for one animal."

"The gold stays right here in Breckenridge, until the railroad picks it up," Jim replied.

When they reached the bank, Jim, Foster, and the others waited until Barnes climbed the steps and pushed open the door. They followed him into the dim interior.

"As far as old Sam goes, don't worry about him," Jim continued. "We've made harder rides than this, lots of times. A good feed while I'm gettin' my chuck, and he'll be rarin' to go. Let's get this money in the safe, then I'll want you to take me to Purdy's. I want to see if you or anyone else recognizes any of those robbers."

It took only a few minutes to deposit the stolen double eagles safely in the Breckenridge Cattlemen's Bank vault. The chore completed, Jim and Dave walked to Purdy's hardware, trailed by an out of breath Barnes. Mort Purdy had laid the dead outlaws out on a back counter. A pimply-faced teenaged clerk kept his eyes on a steady stream of the morbidly curious people who shuffled through the store to stare at the train robbers' bodies. The sound of hammering came from the back room where Purdy, the hardware store proprietor and erstwhile undertaker, was nailing together rough pine boards to make four coffins. Jim shook his head in disgust as he and his companions entered the store. A slight wave of nausea went through him. As a Ranger, he'd many times been forced to take the life of someone, either to save his own or to stop a desperado, but he'd never gotten used to it, and could never understand the fascination so many people had with viewing violent death.

"Hey, watch where you're goin'. Quit pushing," one of the spectators growled as Jim pushed through the throng, shoving aside several men with more than necessary roughness. The man's protest subsided to an inaudible grumbling when he caught the fierce gaze in Jim's glittering blue eyes. With a muttered curse, he stepped aside.

"You recognize any of these jaspers?" Jim asked Foster while they studied the death-frozen features of the four outlaws.

"Can't say as I do," Foster replied, with a shake of his head. "And how about you, Cecil?"

Barnes carefully studied the bodies before replying.

"I'm afraid not, Sheriff. I've never seen them before."

"Kind of funny no one seems to have run across 'em around here before," Jim observed. "They were definitely headed this way. I figure they'd planned on meetin' someone here in town. You're positive you've never seen them before, Dave?"

Foster again carefully scrutinized the bodies.

"I'm dead certain, Jim," he reiterated. "They look like the kind of skunks a man doesn't forget real easy, and I sure wish I could be more help."

"Well, I know that two of them, the swarthy one and the sallow-faced *hombre*, were called Martinez and Houlihan by their pards," Jim explained. "The other two called each other Sloan and Monte. Only problem is, I don't know which one is Houlihan and which is Martinez."

Jim sighed deeply, then shrugged.

"Dave," he said, "I've got to get my horse cared for, then get a wire off to Austin. Captain Trumbull needs to know I've received his message. I also have to tell him I rounded up these renegades and get their descriptions to him. I still need to stop at the hotel and check on some folks from the train. After that, I'll grab some chuck and a couple hours shut-eye before I ride out. I'd appreciate it if you'd stay here for a while, just in case someone recognizes one of these men."

"I'm glad to do that, Jim," Foster agreed. "Like I said, though, I doubt they've ever been here in Breckenridge, and I don't miss too many folks who pass through my town."

"I'm sure you don't, but we can't chance missin' out on any lead," Jim replied.

72

"I reckon you're right," Foster conceded. "Now, to take care of your horse, head on down to Joe's Livery. It's just down the alley from the hotel and the same place I had the other broncs taken, and Joe'll take good care of your mount, and he'll let you bunk in the hayloft, or you can sleep in one of the jail cells 'cause the hotel's full up with all the folks from the train, so those are your only choices, and for your own supper, try the Plainsman Café. Molly over there serves up a decent steak, and a really fine dried apple pie, and a decent cup of coffee."

Foster said all that without even once pausing for breath.

"I appreciate the help, and the advice, Dave," Jim answered. "Much obliged."

Foster halted Jim before he could turn to depart.

"There's just one more thing, Jim. I really wish you'd see Doc Gorlick."

"Mebbe I will do that, when I look in at the hotel," Jim said. "I'll see you before I pull out."

Jim left the hardware store and went back to get Sam, who stood patiently in front of the sheriff's office. He apologized to the big paint, stroking his soft muzzle. "Sorry, bud. I'll get you bedded down for a while."

As usual, Sam responded by burying his nose in Jim's belly, then dropped his head to Jim's hip pocket to beg for a peppermint. Jim gave Sam his expected treat, then climbed into the saddle. He quickly located the livery stable. A young, lanky hostler was lounging in the door. He looked up at Jim's approach.

"Help you, Mister?" he asked.

Jim swung out of the saddle.

"Sure can. You Joe?" he said.

"That'd be me."

"I'm Lieutenant Jim Blawcyzk of the Rangers. Jim'll do just fine. Sheriff Foster tells me you'll take good care of my horse."

"Sure will," Joe said. "Feed, waterin', and a rubdown?" When he reached for Sam's reins, Sam pinned back his ears.

"Sorry, Joe, I wasn't quick enough to warn you Sam's a one man horse."

"So I see."

"Feed and water, make sure he gets a couple quarts of grain and plenty hay," Jim said. "If you'll show me where to put him, I'll rub him down myself. As you already saw, Sam won't tolerate anyone handlin' him but me, so you'll need to get his grain and water before I leave. Far as the hay, a few forkfuls now, then toss some extra in later."

"I can manage that," Joe assured Jim. "I've dealt with ornery cayuses before. I don't mistreat a horse, no matter how cantankerous he might be. Put him in the third stall down on the right."

"Much obliged."

Certain his horse was in capable hands, Jim

headed for the Western Union office, where he composed a telegram for Captain Trumbull. Once the message was mailed, with his belly reminding him he hadn't eaten anything but a few strips of jerky all day, Jim decided to get a quick supper at the Plainsman before stopping at the hotel.

"Hey, Ranger!"

Jim was just opening the door to the café. He pushed the door all the way open and looked down the street to see who was hollering.

Mike Hardy the conductor hurried up the street. His head was encircled by a clean piece of white cloth, which was thicker on the left side of his forehead.

"Mike," Jim said with a broad grin. "I'm sure glad to see you're up and around."

"I can say the same for you," Hardy replied. "I just got word down at the depot you rounded up the men who wrecked and robbed my train. You really killed all of 'em?"

"Only three," Jim answered. "One of them was drilled by his own pardner. Wish it hadn't turned out that way. I'd rather have brought them in alive to stand trial."

"A trial's only a waste of time and money, as far as I'm concerned," Hardy said, his lips compressed to a thin line of bitterness. "Those no-good killers took the lives of innocent women and kids, and my best friend, Chip Danvers. I sure hope they're burnin' in Hades right now."

"I understand your feelin's, but I reckon that's for the good Lord to decide," Jim said. "Look, I was about to get some supper, then stop by the hotel before I grab some shut-eye."

He raised an eyebrow at the conductor.

"Mike, you wouldn't by any chance know James Reasoner of the T&P, would you?"

Hardy shot the Ranger a look of incredulity.

"I sure would know him, although I've only met him a few times. He's a vice-president of the line, in charge of this whole section. Why'd you bring up his name?"

"Because I've gotten orders from Ranger Headquarters to get to Abilene as fast as possible and meet with him," Jim replied. "That's gonna cost me the little bit of sleep I was plannin' on. I'll let my horse rest for a couple of hours, then ride out."

"You've got to meet with Reasoner, huh?" Hardy rubbed his jaw thoughtfully. "Listen, you won't have to make that ride. There's a freight which pulled in just three hours ago. Once some more cars get added to it, it'll roll out, sometime around ten o'clock. It's a slow run, and it makes a couple more stops between here and Abilene, but it'll still be faster than ridin', and a lot easier on you and that paint horse of yours."

Jim gave a rueful chuckle. "I'm not so sure about that. Not after my last train ride, anyway."

Hardy matched Jim's chuckle with a laugh

of his own. "I guess you're right at that," he conceded. "Still, that freight should get you into Abilene by morning. I can have a boxcar added to the train for your horse. Since you're supposed to meet with Mister Reasoner, that won't be a problem. I'm certain you can ride in the caboose along with the crew. What do you say?"

"It's not a bad idea, long as I can convince Sam to get back on a train," Jim replied, then added. "I'll also take the stolen money along. No one'll suspect it's on a whistle stop freight."

"I'll have the orders cut right now," Hardy said.

"No hurry," Jim answered, "I'll need to have Sheriff Foster tell Banker Barnes I'll be picking up the gold later tonight. I'll stop by his office and let him know. By the way, have you eaten yet?"

"Not since noon," Hardy admitted.

"In that case, I wouldn't mind some company with supper. Join me?"

"Sure," Hardy agreed.

Sheriff Foster's assessment of the Plainsman Café was indeed accurate. If pressed, Jim would have admitted that Molly Dodd, the cheerful owner of the eatery, baked an apple pie almost as tasty as his own wife's. After a satisfying supper, Jim parted company with Mike Hardy, who left to order the extra car attached to the overnight freight, and made his way to the Excelsior House.

He was determined to ask about those who'd been injured in the train wreck before boarding the freight for Abilene.

As with so many frontier hotels, the name was the only thing grand about the Excelsior House. The building was a sagging, two-story affair, badly in need of paint both inside and out. The clerk at the desk yawned as Jim walked in.

"Full up," he said.

"Don't want a room. Just tell me where to find Doc Gorlick."

"He's in there." The clerk waved a hand at a door that opened onto the lobby, but entered into no ordinary hotel room.

"Thanks," Jim said, and walked to the door. He stood still for a moment, then knocked.

"Enter," came an order.

A white-haired man sat at the desk. He glanced up when Jim entered, a harried look on his face.

"What can I do for you?" he grumbled. Then he noticed the bloodstain on Jim's shirt. "Let me guess. A gunshot wound. Well, don't just stand there. Get that shirt off. Let's have a look."

"That can wait," Jim replied. "You're Doctor Gorlick?"

"I am indeed . . . Doctor Eugene Gorlick, and I'm far too busy to play games," the physician said. "If you want me to treat that wound, sit on the table and get out of that shirt. If not, get out of here and stop wasting my time. As far as I'm concerned, if you cowpokes insist on shooting each other up, at least do a proper job of it and shoot yourselves dead. That would save me a lot of trouble, and give me much more time for the patients who truly deserve my attention."

"I agree about the cowboys. It'd also save me a lot of trouble if some of 'em would aim straighter and do just that," Jim answered with a trace of irritation in his voice. "I'm not here to be patched up anyway. I want to check on the passengers from the train, particularly a cowboy named Cummings, also a young woman named Lottie Parker, and her daughter."

"What's your interest in them?" Gorlick said, quarrelsome as ever. Then his voice trailed off when he saw the badge on Jim's chest for the first time.

"I was ridin' on that train," Jim said. His voice was soft, but it had hard edges.

"My apologies, Ranger," Gorlick answered. "I didn't mean what I just said. I'm merely tired from working nonstop since the injured arrived. I heard about what you did. I understand I won't be treating the men who destroyed the train."

"No apologies necessary, Doc," Jim reassured him. "I'm plumb worn out myself. I just wanted to check on the folks before I head out. So, if you'll just tell me where I can find Pete or Lottie . . ."

"I did mean one thing I said," Gorlick

interrupted. "From the size of that bloodstain on your shirt, you must have gotten a pretty good slice taken out of you. That bruise on your temple is pretty ugly, too. You're not leaving this room until I've taken care of your wounds."

Gorlick pushed himself up from his chair, his dark eyes snapping. He was on the short side, with a good-sized stomach pushing out his white shirt. He exuded a quiet confidence, along with a no-nonsense manner.

Jim complied. "You're the doc," he said with a grin. He shrugged out of his vest and shirt and sat on the edge of the table. Gorlick gave a low whistle when he saw the huge bruise across Jim's ribs.

"Are you sure you didn't get *hit* by that train?" he asked, and began to probe Jim's side with his fingertips.

"Feels like it," Jim admitted. He flinched when Gorlick touched a particularly tender spot. He gritted his teeth when Gorlick pressed it again.

"Well, it appears you were real lucky. I don't feel any broken ribs. Now, let's see about that bullet hole."

Gorlick began to unwrap Jim's makeshift bandage. He had to peel it away from where dried blood had it stuck to Jim's flesh. He frowned as he examined the wound.

"Ranger, you should have had medical

treatment well before today," he snapped. "It's amazing this wound isn't infected."

"Thanks for the compliment about my doctoring," Jim said, with a laugh.

"This isn't a laughing matter, Ranger . . ." Gorlick hesitated. "You know, you never did give me your name."

"It's Jim Blawcyzk, pronounced BLUH-zhick. Officially, Lieutenant James J. Blawcyzk, if you need that for your records. Last name is spelled b-l-a-w-c-y-z-k."

"Lieutenant, you'll never live to make captain if you keep neglecting bullet wounds in yourself like you did this one."

"I've been kinda busy," Jim retorted.

"That's been the epitaph of many a man," the irascible Gorlick shot back. "Well, let me see if I can repair this damage."

Gorlick went to the stove, from which he removed a pan of hot water. He soaked a cloth in the scalding liquid.

"This will hurt," he warned, as he applied the cloth to Jim's side.

Jim sat quietly while Gorlick swabbed dirt, dried blood, and bits of flesh from the wound, but grimaced in pain when Gorlick doused it with a carbolic solution.

"I'm going to bind that bullet hole and your ribs tightly," he explained, "just in case there's a cracked rib I missed."

Jim grunted when the bandage was pulled tight. "I need to breathe, Doc," he protested.

"You will, at least until you stop a bullet for good," Gorlick muttered as if talking to himself. "There, that's finished. Now, let me take a look at your head."

He pulled several splinters from Jim's temple, then dressed the wound and covered it with a clean square of gauze, wrapping a strip of cloth around Jim's head to hold it in place.

"I've done all I can," Gorlick announced. "You can get back into your shirt. Now, you'll need bed rest, for at least two days."

"Sorry, Doc," Jim answered. "I've got to be in Abilene by morning."

"You can't even think of that," Gorlick objected. "You've lost a lot of blood, and you're obviously exhausted. I'll have a cot made up for you, and I insist you make use of it."

"I can't," Jim reiterated. "I've got orders, and a seat on the freight pullin' out later tonight. So, just tell me how much I owe you, and where I can find either Pete or Mrs. Parker."

Gorlick threw up his hands. "I give up. If you want to kill yourself, that's your prerogative. Two dollars will make us even. Get dressed, and I'll take you to your friends."

Once Jim had his shirt back on, Doctor Gorlick led him up a worn flight of stairs, to Room 10 on the second floor. He paused at the door and knocked once.

"Mister Cummings, there's someone here to see you, if you're ready for some company," he called.

"Sure, Doc. Send 'em in," Pete responded.

"You can go in now, Lieutenant. Just don't stay overlong," Gorlick cautioned. "And I still wish you'd reconsider, take my advice, and rest for a few days."

"There's nothing I'd like better, but I just can't," Jim replied. "Thanks again for patchin' me up."

"It was probably a waste of time," Gorlick grumbled. "Good-bye, Lieutenant, and good luck to you."

"*Adios*, Doc." Jim turned, opened the door, and stepped into Room 10.

"Ranger," Pete exclaimed, when he caught sight of Jim. "We'd heard you were back, and had caught up with those sons of—," Pete caught himself. "—um, sidewinders." The reason he had stopped before completing his oath was plain. To Jim's surprise, Lottie Parker was also in the room, and seated next to Pete's bed. She rose from the chair, came over to Jim, and gave him a kiss on the cheek. Jim blushed.

"Don't look so surprised, Jim," Lottie said, with a hearty laugh. "After what Pete did for me and Sarah, I just can't leave him to fend for himself, at least not until he's up and around."

"Hello, Lottie. Howdy, Pete," Jim finally managed to say. "How are y'all doin'?"

"I'm just fine, Jim. So's Sarah," Lottie replied. "She went to fetch some water, so she'll be back shortly. She'll be so pleased to see you."

"How about you, Pete?" Jim questioned the lanky cowboy, who was stretched out on his bed, with his right leg bound in a splint.

"I'll be okay, Jim," Pete answered. "Just gonna be laid up for a spell. I've got the two prettiest nurses in all of Texas, though."

"Oh, go on with you, Peter Cummings." This time, Lottie blushed.

"It's the truth, and you know it," Pete retorted. "In fact, here's the other one now."

Sarah entered the room, carrying a pitcher of water.

"Ranger Jim!" She almost dropped the pitcher.

"Hi Sarah." Jim gave her a smile. "You been takin' good care of your Mom, and that ugly old *hombre* over there?"

"Mister Pete's not ugly," Sarah said, her nose in the air.

Pete laughed. "That's a right smart girl there, Jim. She's got good eyes, too."

"She's only about six, so she's just too young to know any better," Jim shot back. "Seriously, though. Y'all gonna be okay?"

"As Pete said, Jim, we're doing just fine. Sarah

and I have a room across the hall, so we can hear him call if he needs anything," Lottie explained.

"And Mister Pete's going to take us home to his ranch once his leg's better," Sarah piped up.

"Is that a fact?" Jim said, smiling.

This time it was Pete who flushed bright red.

"It sure is, Jim," he answered. "Lottie's got nowhere else to go. She was hopin' to find work in El Paso. You know how hard that can be for a woman, especially . . . well, you know the kind of work she would have been offered. I know it's kind of sudden, but Lottie and I have talked this over, and she's agreed to think about marryin' me."

"That's wonderful news," Jim said. "I hope you'll both be very happy. Sarah, promise me you'll keep an eye on Pete and your mom."

"I will, Ranger Jim, really. I promise," Sarah said.

"Fine. Now come over here, and give me a big ol' hug."

"Is that all right, Mommy?" Sarah asked.

"It's fine, darling," her mother said.

Sarah ran to Jim and wrapped her arms around his neck.

"Whoa. Don't choke me to death," Jim said, laughing. "Save the rest of your hugs for your mom and Pete." He disentangled himself from Sarah's arms.

"What about you, Jim?" Lottie asked. "What

are your plans? Will you be staying in town for a while?"

"I'm afraid not," Jim replied. "I got orders to get to Abilene as soon as possible. The railroad's found space for me and Sam on the next train out. We're leavin' around ten tonight."

"Are you certain you'll be all right?" Pete questioned, thrusting his chin at the bullet hole in Jim's blood-stained shirt. "Looks like you had a mite of trouble with those *hombres*."

"It's not all that bad," Jim reassured him. "A bullet sliced along my ribs. Doc Gorlick patched me up just fine." He paused. "Even though he's a grumpy old cuss, ain't he? Besides, I'm in a lot better shape than those train robbers."

"Don't let the hard crust fool you, Jim," Lottie advised. "I'm positive Doctor Gorlick has a heart of gold under that tough exterior."

"If he does, then he's got it well hidden," Jim replied. "Anyway, I'd better get movin'. I just wanted to stop by and say '*Adios*' to all of you before I left. I'm going to try and grab an hour or two of shut-eye."

"Well, if you ever get down San Angelo way, you be sure and look us up," Pete ordered. "I own the Box PC, a few miles south of town."

"So you're more than just a grub-line ridin' cowpoke," Jim said.

"Reckon I am at that," Pete admitted.

"I'll do that," Jim promised. "That goes both

ways. If you ever find yourselves in Austin, stop by Ranger Headquarters. Cap'n Trumbull will let you know if I'm around. I've got a small horse ranch just outside town, in San Leanna, along with my wife, Julia, and son, Charlie. We'd be more than happy to have y'all visit. Don't worry about not findin' me at home. Julia runs the place, and does a far better job of it than I ever could."

"Then that's settled," Lottie stated, hands on her hips. "Jim, you'd better get that sleep. Pete, it's also high time you got some, too."

"We're not even married yet, and already she's orderin' me around." Pete grinned at his own joke.

"Better get used to it, cowboy," Jim laughed.

"That's it. Out of here. Now!" Lottie ordered.

"Yes, *ma'am*," Jim said, and with a wave of his hand to Pete and a pat to the top of Sarah's head, he left.

On the way back to the livery stable, Jim stopped in at the sheriff's office. Dave Foster gave him a cup of coffee and assured him Cecil Barnes would have the stolen gold ready. As they'd both expected, no one who'd looked at the dead outlaws admitted to recognizing any of them.

"Doesn't really matter anyway, Jim," Foster said. "You brought 'em all in, and they won't be botherin' anybody ever again."

"I guess you're right," Jim agreed. "Besides,

with any luck, Cap'n Trumbull will be able to match their descriptions to some names."

"You want some more coffee before you go?" Foster asked, hefting the battered pot.

"No, thanks anyway," Jim declined. "I'd better get some sleep."

He stood and yawned, then drained the last of his cup.

"I'll see you later, Dave."

"I'll meet you at the bank," Foster replied.

At the livery stable, Jim checked on Sam and gave him a peppermint. He got his blanket roll off the saddle and unrolled it in a corner of the hayloft. In moments he was asleep, not stirring until Joe, the hostler, awakened him. Jim gathered his gear, roused his horse, saddled up, and rode the short distance to the bank.

Sheriff Foster, with his shotgun cradled under his arm, was waiting for him. When Jim dismounted, Foster nodded at the bank door.

"Cecil's waitin' inside," he said.

"Fine, then let's get this over with," Jim answered. "The fewer people who know what we're doin', the better."

Both men stepped into the bank.

"Lieutenant," Cecil Barnes called. His voice trembled. "The money is all ready for you. I must say, I'll be very happy to have it out of my bank."

"Well, I've gotta admit I'll be even happier once

I get it to Abilene," Jim replied. "I appreciate your help, Mister Barnes. Much obliged."

"Always happy to help the Texas Rangers," Barnes said.

"We'd best get those bags down to the station right now," Foster pointed out.

"I reckon you're right, Dave," Jim agreed. Grunting, he hoisted two of the gold-laden saddlebags onto his shoulders. Foster took the remaining pair.

"These things are heavy," Foster complained.

"Boy howdy, that's certain," Jim said. "Thanks again, Mister Barnes."

"You're welcome. Good luck to you, Lieutenant," Barnes answered.

Mike Hardy was at the depot when Jim and Foster arrived. He introduced Jim to the freight's crew.

"The boxcar's all ready for your horse, Jim . . . the last one, just before the caboose," he directed. "I figured you'd want him as close to you as possible."

"You figured exactly right, Mike," Jim answered. "Which is why I'm gonna ride in the car with Sam."

"You're sure about that?" Hardy questioned. "You'd be lots more comfortable in the caboose."

"I'm not lettin' this gold out of my sight until I reach Abilene," Jim explained. He patted the saddlebags, which now were lying across Sam's withers. "Don't worry about me. I'll be just fine."

Hardy shook his head. "Okay. Long as you're certain. You'd better get on board. The train's about ready to pull out."

"Sure." Jim shook hands with Hardy and Foster. "Thanks for everything, both of you."

"We should be thanking you, Jim," Hardy responded. "You just take care of yourself, hear?"

"Count on that," Jim said. "Dave," he continued, "if you should happen to come up with a name for any of those renegades, wire me in Abilene."

"Will do," Foster promised, as they reached the boxcar. "*Adios*, Jim."

"*Adios*, Dave, Mike."

Hardy slid open the boxcar's door. Sam jerked back, pulling hard against the reins, not wanting to climb the ramp into the car.

Jim reassured the horse. "It's all right, Sam. I'm right here with you." With a final snort of protest, Sam lunged into the car.

Jim piled his gear and the gold-laden money-bags in a corner of the car, unsaddled Sam, took his bridle off, then rolled out his blankets and set the saddle where he could use it as a pillow. He stretched out on the hay-strewn floor, and before the train had even rolled away from the station, he was fast asleep.

CHAPTER SIX

Completely exhausted, Jim slept almost the entire journey to Abilene, stirring only when the train stopped to take on more cars or water. He at last awakened when the sun rose and now, as the freight rolled into Abilene, he had Sam saddled and bridled, and the money-laden saddlebags draped over his withers. They were ready to get off the minute the train reached the platform and the ramp was lowered.

Sam impatiently nudged the door with his nose as the train chugged slowly up to the station.

Jim laughed. "Easy, bud. I'm every bit as eager to get off this thing as you are. It'll only be a few more minutes."

Finally, with the clanking of couplers and hissing of released steam, the freight rolled to a halt. Jim slid open the boxcar's door, and as soon as a ramp was in place led his horse onto the platform.

"Thanks for the ride," he called to the brakeman.

"Any time, Ranger," the trainman shouted back, with a smile and wave.

Jim looked around, surprised at the changes in the railroad town since his last visit two years previous. An imposing, two-story brick structure replaced the crude wooden station Jim recalled. It even had a clock tower, the clock in which was just chiming eight.

"Town sure has grown, Sam," Jim remarked. He let the paint dip his muzzle into a water trough in front of the station. Main Street, lined with brick buildings and stores with plate glass windows, was bustling. Jim draped Sam's reins over a hitchrail.

"Wait here, Sam," he ordered. "I'll be back to hunt you up a stall and some feed quick as I can."

Jim lifted the saddlebags containing the gold from Sam's withers and put them onto a luggage cart, straining with the effort. Pushing his way, with the cart in tow, through the heavy carved-oak doors and into the station's main waiting room, he worked his way through the milling throng of passengers and up to an iron-grilled ticket window. The agent behind the counter eyed Jim dubiously.

"Help you, Mister?" he asked, barely able to hide the disdain in his voice.

"I need to know where to find Mr. Reasoner," Jim answered.

"You mean James Reasoner, one of the vice-presidents of this railroad?" The agent's voice took on a tone of disbelief.

"Unless you're hidin' another James Reasoner around here," Jim sarcastically replied. "Mister,

I don't have time to waste. I just spent the entire night ridin' on a slow freight so I could keep an appointment with Mr. Reasoner. I don't think he'd appreciate bein' told you kept me waitin'."

"All right, all right," the agent said with a shrug. "His office is on the second floor. Turn right at the top of the stairs, and go to the end of the hallway."

"Fine. You see this cart?"

"Yeah, what about it?"

"I need you to hold it behind your counter until I get back. Don't let anyone near it. Get someone else to keep an eye on it if need be."

The look in Jim's eyes and tone of his voice warned the clerk he would brook no argument.

"I'll make sure of it. Lemme just call another man over. Andy," the clerk called. Another agent hustled up.

"Yeah, Joe?"

"This man has an appointment with Mr. Reasoner. He needs us to watch his luggage until he returns."

"Not a problem," Andy said. "Your things will be safe until you come back, Mister."

He picked up the cart's handle and pulled it behind the counter.

"Thanks for your help," Jim said. He turned on his heels, leaving the agents staring at his broad back. He strode swiftly across the terminal and up the stairs, then through a door with "Texas and Pacific Regional Offices" in gold leaf on its window.

When he entered the room, a prim secretary glanced up from behind her desk. She ran her gaze contemptuously over Jim's dirty, unshaven face and rumpled, soot-stained clothes. Her eyes widened when she noticed the bullet hole in the side of his shirt.

"May I help you, Sir?" she asked, her voice frosty.

"I'm here to see James Reasoner," Jim explained.

"Do you have an appointment?" the secretary asked. "Mr. Reasoner is a very busy man."

"I'm afraid I don't," Jim admitted. "However, I believe he'll see me. I'm Lieutenant Blawcyzk of the Texas Rangers."

He reached in his shirt's left breast pocket, pulled out his badge, and pinned to his vest.

"I'll see if Mr. Reasoner is available."

The secretary disappeared behind a door marked "Private", then returned a few moments later.

"Mr. Reasoner will see you now." She sniffed in disdain. "Please go right in."

"Thank you," Jim said, with his crooked smile. He stepped around her desk and into James Reasoner's office. Reasoner rose from behind his desk as soon as Jim entered, extended his hand, and took Jim's in a firm grip. The Texas and Pacific vice-president was a stocky, balding man, with a full beard covering the lower half of his face. He peered at Jim through a pair of thick spectacles.

"Lieutenant Blawcyzk," he said, "Thank you for coming. I hope I pronounced your name correctly."

"Close enough," Jim answered. "And you're welcome. Not that I had much choice."

"My orders were specific. The recovered money from the El Paso Limited is downstairs behind the ticket counter, being watched by two of your agents. They don't know what's in the bags, but assured me the contents would be safe. Now, would you mind telling me what this is all about?"

"Not at all, Lieutenant," Reasoner answered. "However, I want to have Chet Dobson, my chief detective, present when we have our discussion, and he won't be available for at least an hour. He's returning on one of the work trains."

Reasoner paused, studying Jim's gaunt, beard-stubbled face and his torn, stained clothing.

"You certainly look as if you can use some time to rest and clean up, if you don't mind my saying so, Lieutenant. There's a barbershop across the street and an excellent café right here in the terminal. Why don't you get a bath and shave, if you desire, then breakfast. Tell Thomas at the café to put your meal on my account. Why

95

don't we plan on meeting back here at, say, ten o'clock? That will allow you plenty of time for a leisurely meal."

"What about the gold?"

"I'll handle that personally. Don't you concern yourself with it any longer. Please, accept my offer. Get the rest and food you need."

"That's mighty decent of you. I've got to care for my horse, then I'll take you up on that offer," Jim replied. Normally, he would be chafing with impatience at the delay, but he could sense Reasoner was not a man to be rushed. Besides, he was indeed famished, and desperately wanted to scrape off some of the trail dust coating his body. He also needed to replace his clothes, especially the bullet-torn and bloodstained shirt.

"You might not be so grateful, once you hear the reason I asked Captain Trumbull for your help," Reasoner said. "However, let's not worry about that for the moment. There's a fine livery stable two blocks down. They'll take excellent care of your mount. I'll see you back here at ten."

"I'll be here," Jim assured him. "You can bet your hat on it."

Forty minutes later, Sam was settled in a clean stall and munching on hay, while Jim, freshly barbered and shaved, soaked in a big zinc tub full of hot, soapy water.

Mebbe I'll just make that meeting at eleven instead, he thought, as he settled more deeply into the soothing liquid.

At precisely nine fifty-eight, Jim, dressed in a fresh shirt and jeans which the barber had procured for him, his boots and Stetson brushed as clean as possible, returned to the Texas and Pacific's offices.

"May I help you, sir?" Reasoner's secretary once again asked him, this time unable to completely mask the admiration in her eyes, as she ran her gaze over Jim's rugged form.

"Aw, ma'am, I couldn't have looked *that* bad before," Jim drawled. He gave her a crooked grin.

"Lieutenant Blawcyzk!" the flustered secretary exclaimed, when she recognized his smile. "Mr. Reasoner told me you'd be back at ten. I'm so sorry. It's just that . . ."

"I know, ma'am," Jim broke in. "I reckon I did look like somethin' the coyotes had been chewin' on when I first came in. There's no need to apologize."

"I apologize anyway," she replied. "You go right on in. Mr. Reasoner is waiting."

"Thank you, ma'am."

Jim headed for Reasoner's office, aware of the woman's admiring gaze on his back.

Reasoner greeted Jim when he stepped into the

office. "Welcome back, Lieutenant. I appreciate a man who's prompt. I'd like you to meet Chet Dobson, the Texas and Pacific's chief detective and investigator. He's already delivered the money you recovered to the Abilene National Bank."

"Lieutenant, I'm pleased to meet you," Dobson said, as they shook hands. Dobson's dark brown eyes seemed to be taking Jim's measure, despite the smile that showed beneath a huge, drooping walrus mustache. Of blocky build, Dobson gave Jim a solid grip when shaking hands, but his florid face said perhaps he enjoyed john barleycorn somewhat.

"Same here," Jim answered, returning Dobson's gaze. "But, if you don't mind, I'd really like to know why I'm here."

"Of course," Reasoner agreed. "Please, have a seat."

He indicated a red leather armchair in the corner, then waved at a decanter and glasses on a heavy walnut sideboard. "Would you care for a cigar, or perhaps a brandy?"

Jim politely declined. "No, thank you."

"Fine . . . Chet?"

"I don't mind if I do, James," Dobson accepted. He chose a cigar from the rosewood humidor on Reasoner's desk, then poured himself a generous tumbler-full of brandy from the cut-crystal decanter. Dobson took a seat in the chair opposite

Jim's, while Reasoner settled in the thick, green leather chair behind his desk. He also chose a cigar and lit it, taking a long puff and exhaling a ring of bluish smoke toward the ceiling.

"Lieutenant," Reasoner began, studying the ash on his cigar. "I want to thank you again for all you've done for the Texas and Pacific."

"I was just in the right place, that's all," Jim answered. "Rest was merely doing my job."

"Nonetheless, if you hadn't been on that train, then followed those outlaws so diligently, I have no doubt they would have gotten away with their crime," Reasoner responded. "Now, I am positive you believe that robbery was an isolated incident. Let me assure you it was not . . . which is why I asked Captain Trumbull to order you here."

"I don't quite follow you."

Dobson broke in. "What Mr. Reasoner is saying is that the wrecking and robbery of the El Paso Limited was merely the latest in a string of manmade accidents and thefts. All plaguing our railroad. We have been trying to handle the problem internally, but with little success."

Reasoner continued the account. "A couple of weeks ago, we requested Ranger protection for our crews building a new spur from Big Spring to Twist, and that request was granted. When I received news of the destruction of the Limited and learned you had been on that train, I immediately wired your commanding officer and requested your assistance. Captain Trumbull replied almost as quickly, sending me this message, which I am in turn to pass on to you."

Reasoner picked up a yellow Western Union flimsy from his desk and handed it to Jim, who read:

Request for Lt Blawcyzk's assistance investigation of T&P incidents granted STOP On his arrival have Lt take charge of men previously assigned STOP Capt H Trumbull Texas Rangers STOP

Once Jim looked up from the telegram, Reasoner continued, "Your apprehension of those criminals tells me I was right in following my instincts. However, I'm sure you have more than a few questions. Let me explain first, then Chet or I will be more than happy to tell you what we know."

"Fine," Jim said.

"As I mentioned, Lieutenant, we are building a spur line from Big Spring to Twist. Eventually, we hope to continue it northward to Denver. Ever since we began construction of that line, we have been plagued with problems. Chet, would you give the lieutenant some details, please."

"At first, there were just minor incidents of vandalism, nothing we couldn't be certain were anything other than accidents," Dobson explained. "However, the problems increased, not only on the new spur line, but all along our

100

system, from Dallas clear through to El Paso. Derailments—some caused by tracks being torn up, others by switches being thrown. Robberies—but none as serious as the wrecking of the El Paso Limited. In short, we believe someone is deliberately attempting to put the Texas and Pacific Railroad out of business."

"In response to our first request, Captain Trumbull assigned four Rangers to protect our construction crews working on the new line," Reasoner continued. "Those men are already with the crews, just north of Lamesa. That's where we've established our current construction camp."

"Who are they?" Jim asked.

"A Sergeant McCue, along with Rangers Menendez, Timmons, and Smith," Dobson answered.

"I know the first three. They're good men," Jim replied, smiling inwardly at the thought of being reunited with his former riding pards. "I don't know Ranger Smith, but I'm sure he's a good lawman."

"Yes, and they are indeed doing a fine job of protecting our men," Reasoner agreed. "However, we need an individual who can ferret out the person or persons behind the plot against the T & P. That's why I requested Captain Trumbull to assign you to this case. I don't need to tell you, if we cannot stop these incidents, we could soon be in trouble financially. In fact, we are already having trouble raising additional capital."

"I'll do what I can, but I'll need more information," Jim replied. "First, where in the blue blazes is Twist? I've never heard of it."

"It's a new town, close to the New Mexico and Indian Territory borders," Dobson answered. "It's named after one of our sections. Ranching is doing quite well in the northern Panhandle, so we believe the town will grow rapidly once the rails reach it."

"All right, that makes sense," Jim answered. "Do you have any ideas as to who might want to stop the T&P from completing this line?"

"There are several jerkline freight outfits the new spur will put out of business," Dobson said. "However, none of their owners seem the type that would start trouble. They understand the days of the mule and wagon outfits are numbered."

"I'll still want to talk to them," Jim said.

"I'll have Betty give you a list of their names," Reasoner answered.

"Fine," Jim said. "Anyone else?"

"Some of the landowners objected to our taking their acreage," Dobson explained. "However, the majority of them were satisfied with the price we offered. There were only two or three parcels where we had to invoke eminent domain."

"I'll also need to speak to those men," Jim answered.

"I'll provide you their names, too," Reasoner agreed.

Dobson spoke up. "Mr. Reasoner, several of them have already left the state."

"I'll still want to talk with the ones I can find," Jim said. "Anything else that might be helpful?"

"I don't believe so," Reasoner responded. "Just that we need whoever is behind these attacks stopped, and quickly. I can't emphasize that enough."

"I'll do my best, bet a hat on it," Jim assured him. "I'd like a list of all the incidents, as well as a route map of the new spur line. I'd also appreciate the names of everyone you dealt with in negotiating the route."

"We'll have everything you requested by late this afternoon," Dobson promised.

"That'll do," Jim said. "Once I have the information, I'll ride out to the construction camp. If I push my horse hard, I should make it in three or four days."

"There's no need for that," Reasoner replied. "I'm heading up there by special train tomorrow morning. The men have worked hard, and, despite everything, construction of the line is proceeding far more rapidly than we anticipated, so we are ahead of schedule. With Independence Day being the day after tomorrow, I'm giving the crews a day off with pay, and a bonus. You can ride with Chet and I, which will give us a chance to discuss matters further. And we'll be at our destination by tomorrow afternoon, which will save you a good deal of time, and a lot of wear and tear on yourself and your animal. I'll have the documents you requested on the train with me."

"That will work just fine," Jim said. "What time should we meet?"

"We'll be pulling out at seven."

"Then I'll see you at the station just before seven." Jim turned to leave.

"Not quite so fast, Lieutenant," Reasoner said. "Since you'll be in town until tomorrow, why not join us for supper?"

"Thanks for the invitation. I truly appreciate it, but I'll have to decline. I want to look up the town marshal and have a word with him," Jim said.

"Tyler Todd?" Dobson asked.

"One and the same. He's an old friend of mine. After I see him, I've still got some shut-eye to catch up on."

"Well, then I can't blame you for declining," Reasoner said. "I'll see you in the morning."

"Both of you, I trust," Jim said, gazing directly at Dobson.

"Of course," Dobson agreed. "Why do you ask?"

"Because with Mr. Reasoner carrying cash bonuses for the construction workers, I fully expect trouble tomorrow," Jim said.

Dobson objected. "We've taken every possible precaution. Very few people know about that cash."

"One more person than Mr. Reasoner is one too many. Bet a hat on it," Jim answered. "I'll also want the names of everyone who knows about that bonus money. And where they are right now, if you know."

"Surely you're not implying—?" Dobson protested.

"I'm not implying anything, at least not yet," Jim answered. "If you need to reach me today, get in touch with Marshal Todd. He'll know where to find me."

After a quiet supper with his old friend, Marshal Tyler Todd, Jim walked back up Main Street toward the Drover's Hotel, where he had taken a room.

"Gotta stop and check on Sam before I turn in," he said aloud. "Better make sure he hasn't torn off the hostler's head."

Jim stopped abruptly. Just as he did, a bullet whined past his face to shatter a window in the harness maker's shop.

Jim dove to his belly and yanked out his Colt as another bullet ripped through the air over his head. He'd seen a flash in the alley across the street, so he emptied his sixgun into it. The last shot brought a grunt of pain, followed by the sound of footsteps running away. Jim leaped to his feet, crouched low, and ran for the alley's mouth, ejecting spent shells and reloading as he went. He ducked behind a rain barrel at the corner and peered into the darkness, listening intently.

Hearing no further movement in the alleyway, Jim left the shelter of the barrel. He edged his way along a wall and into the alley, fully expecting a barrage of slugs to come ripping in his direction at any moment. Finally, he reached the far end of the alley, where the dim starlight revealed a trampled patch of ground, as well as several dark spots, damp and glistening.

A shout rang out from the street.

"What's goin' on back there? You in the alley, toss out your gun and come out with your hands over your head!"

Jim breathed a sigh of relief when he recognized Marshal Todd's voice. "It's all right, Ty," he called. "It's me, Jim. I'm the only one in here, now. Keep those folks out."

The marshal pushed his way through the crowd that had gathered at the mouth of the alleyway. He slid his Navy Colt back into its holster.

"Jim?" A match flared, and a lantern's soft glow soon penetrated the alley's gloom. "What the devil's goin' on?"

Jim answered when Todd reached him, keeping his voice low. "Someone took a couple of potshots at me, Ty."

"You all right?" Todd asked.

"I'm fine." Jim pointed at the drops of blood and the footprints that disappeared into the packed dirt. "Appears like I might've winged the *hombre*, but he's not hit bad. He took off."

"Well, I'll notify Doc Chambers, just in case some jigger shows up at his door wantin' a bullet dug outta his hide," Todd replied. "You got any idea who might be tryin' to gun you?"

"*Quien sabe*," Jim shrugged. "Could've been somebody attemptin' a robbery, or mebbe even a drunk just lettin' off steam."

"More likely someone who wants you dead." Todd spit a long stream of tobacco juice into the dust.

Jim grinned. "Kinda goes with the territory when you're a lawman."

"I reckon you're right about that," Todd agreed, shaking his head. "Well, as you said, there's nothing more to be done here. I'll break up the crowd. You sure you're okay?"

"Never better, bet a hat on it," Jim said. "We still on for breakfast?"

"Coffee'll be on."

"Good. I'll enjoy drinking it."

"Don't get yourself gut-shot fulla holes first," Todd said. "Coffee'll likely leak right out if you do."

In his room, Jim quickly knelt to say his evening prayers, undressed, and slipped under the covers. But, despite his exhaustion, sleep refused to come. He just lay there, stretched out on the bed, staring up at the ceiling.

Who'd want to take a shot at me? Could've been somebody I've had a run-in with before. A lawman never knows when he's gonna cross paths with someone who'd like nothing better than to get even by puttin' a slug in his back. But his instincts said that wasn't the case. He'd kept his Ranger star pretty well concealed since arriving in Abilene, and revealed his identity to just a few people. In addition, he'd only been in Abilene once before, and that was over two years ago. It was unlikely anyone would remember him from that visit. Still, word spread fast in any frontier town, especially if the ticket agents or Reasoner's secretary were gossips. The freight's crew, after a few drinks, had probably also spread the word about a Texas Ranger on their train.

Reckon I wasn't as careful about my I.D. as I thought.

Finally, unable to shake the nagging feeling that someone had pointed him out and wanted him dead before he ever reached Lamesa, Jim fell into a troubled sleep.

CHAPTER SEVEN

"Last time you'll have to ride a cattle car, Sam, I promise you," Jim reassured his horse when they reached the Texas and Pacific yards early the next morning. "Let's find out where our train is at."

"Lieutenant, over here." Chet Dobson hailed Jim as he rounded the back of the depot. He pointed to a short train waiting at the freight platform, its locomotive idly dribbling smoke and steam. One boxcar's door stood open.

"That car's all ready for your horse. Once he's loaded, Mr. Reasoner would like you to join him for breakfast in his private car."

"Reckon I don't have to ask which one that is," Jim responded with a chuckle. The last car on the train was painted a deep maroon, trimmed in gold leaf, and lettered "Private". "By the way, Chet," Jim said, "since we'll be working together, just call me Jim. It's a lot simpler."

Dobson laughed. "Sure, I'll do that. And you're right about the car."

"Whadda'ya let's get Sam loaded."

Jim led his paint into the boxcar. He slipped the bridle from Sam's head, but left the saddle in place, cinch tight.

"Sorry, pard," he said as he gave Sam a

peppermint, "but I need you ready in case of trouble." He patted Sam's shoulder, then left him to munch on the hay stacked in the corner. Just before he exited the car, he turned and went back. He slid his Winchester from the saddleboot, then took a box of extra cartridges from his saddlebags. On the platform, Chet Dobson gave him a knowing look.

"You still expectin' trouble, Jim?"

"I'm just about ready to bet my hat on it," Jim replied as he slid the door of Sam's car shut. "That fancy private car is an open invitation to just about every renegade in the territory."

Dobson sighed. "You're telling me. I tried to talk Mr. Reasoner out of using it. But he's giving the men a big celebration, and besides, it's the Fourth of July, so he wouldn't even consider any other car."

"Well, let's just hope we're both wrong," Jim answered. He studied the train as they walked along the tracks. There were several flatcars carrying equipment and supplies, then two boxcars, including the one holding his horse, a passenger coach, and finally the private car.

"Here we are," Dobson announced. He climbed the iron steps and opened the door to Reasoner's private coach. Jim entered to find three men, besides James Reasoner, in the car.

Reasoner rose from a dark leather sofa.

"Lieutenant," he said, "Welcome to my home

110

away from home." Then his eyes narrowed when he spotted the rifle in Jim's left hand.

"Is that gun really necessary?"

"My orders are to keep the Texas and Pacific from having any more trouble," Jim replied, "so the answer is yes."

"As you wish, although I don't believe we'll have trouble," Reasoner said, with a shrug. "I'd like to introduce these men to you. This is Theodore McGarry, our paymaster. Joshua Briggs, our bookkeeper. And Sol Morris, our chief surveyor. Gentlemen, Lieutenant Blawcyzk of the Texas Rangers."

The T&P men and Jim exchanged pleasantries as Reasoner turned to a uniformed woman who stood behind a dark cherrywood counter, which ran half the length of the car.

"Effie, please give the lieutenant a cup of coffee, then you may begin to serve," he ordered. His tone of voice made it clear that he was speaking to someone below his station.

"Yes, sir, Mr. Reasoner. George has every-thing prepared. I'll have your meal shortly." She poured a bone china cup full of coffee and handed it to Jim, then disappeared behind a door at the far end of the car.

As the train slowly chugged out of the station, Jim settled into a red velvet armchair. He glanced around with frank admiration at the sumptuous surroundings. The car was paneled in hand-carved, highly polished walnut, and a gilt and crystal chandelier hung from the center of the ceiling. The furnishings were upholstered in either deep red velvet or leather, and a thick Persian rug covered the floor.

"How do you like it, Lieutenant?" Reasoner asked.

"Better'n most hotels I've stayed in," Jim said.

"It is a *bit* ostentatious," Reasoner admitted. "However, since I must be on the rails most of the time and I refuse to bring my wife and daughters into such unsettled territory, I try to make myself as comfortable as possible."

"I'd say you succeeded."

"Indeed. That's what Livia, my wife, says also. Are you married, Lieutenant?"

"Yes," Jim answered. "I've got a wife and eight year old son, back home near Austin."

"Then you know how lonely it can be when you're away from home."

"I sure do," Jim replied. He took another swallow of his coffee. "But, I chose my lifestyle, and luckily Julia and Charlie understand. Plus, Sam's good company. I can talk to him, and that helps."

"Then we're both fortunate men," Reasoner said. "Ah, here comes Effie with our meal. We'll discuss the situation and our plans while we eat."

After breakfast and over Reasoner's objections,

Jim settled himself in the forward coach with Chet Dobson. Other railroaders occupied the car, some dozing, others gazing out the windows. Theodore McGarry and Joshua Briggs were also present, huddled over company ledgers. Jim and Dobson occupied themselves going over the names and documents Jim had requested.

With a forefinger, Jim tapped the list of freighting companies that the new spur would put out of business. "Anyone in particular in this bunch strike you as the type to stir up trouble, Chet?" he asked.

"Not really," Dobson replied. "A few of 'em made some noise, but they pretty much realized they were fighting a losing battle. Most of them are ready to pull up stakes." He pulled a cigar out of his vest pocket, lit it, and leaned back, thoughtfully blowing smoke rings. "To answer your next question, I don't believe any of the landowners we displaced are behind this trouble either. The T&P offered them a fair price for their land and most of them were happy to accept our offer."

"You said most of them," Jim pointed out.

"Yes, most. But, you have to understand, they were all small farmers or ranchers. None of them, it seems to me, would have the resources, in cash or manpower, to take on the Texas and Pacific. Same goes for the freighters."

"But someone is," Jim argued. "And you say

the trouble didn't start until after construction on the line to Twist began."

"That's correct." Dobson took a long puff on his cigar. "Truthfully, I don't have the faintest idea who it might be."

"Well, mebbe I can come up with somethin'," Jim said. "Especially now that things have gotten kind of personal."

"What do you mean?" Dobson asked.

"Someone took a couple of shots at me from an alley last night. I don't think it was a coincidence. Whoever it was didn't want me gettin' on this train."

"You think there's someone on the inside behind this?"

"Seems there would almost have to be. You can't tell me the thought hasn't crossed your mind."

"No, I sure can't," Dobson admitted. "I've had that feeling all along."

"Which will make our job even harder," Jim replied. He picked up another file. "Let's keep plowin' through this."

Jim and Dobson spent several hours going over the papers Reasoner had provided, then Jim leaned back in his seat, stretched, and thumbed his Stetson back off his forehead. With a frown, he glanced down once again at the route map of the new spur.

"Chet," he observed, "Seems kinda funny to

114

me the T&P is runnin' this spur line out of Big Spring. The more direct route would have been northwest from Abilene, or even Sweetwater. Goin' by way of Big Spring, you're talkin' at least an extra seventy-five miles."

"That's how it would look at first glance," Dobson conceded. "However, from what I understand, the terrain on this route is flatter, so there's less of a grade running the line due north out of Big Spring. Also, we won't have to find a pass or run a tunnel through the Caprock."

"That shouldn't have been much of a challenge," Jim noted. "There's plenty of canyons which cut through the Caprock. Your surveyors should have been able to find a reasonable route without much trouble."

Jim was thoroughly familiar with the Caprock, the two hundred fifty plus miles long north-south escarpment that abruptly separated the high plains of northwest Texas from the lower lands to the east and south.

"It seems that way to me, too," Dobson agreed. "But I'm no construction engineer. There were also a couple of other factors involved."

"I'd bet my hat one was money," Jim said.

"That's right," Dobson admitted. "First of all, word got out that the Texas and Pacific was considering a route from Abilene to Twist, and the price of land along the proposed right-of-way exploded."

"Which made it more economically feasible to use a route out of Big Spring."

"Mighty fancy way of saying it was cheaper, Jim, but yes."

"What else?"

"Big Spring's politicians offered the T&P some mighty attractive reasons to build out of there."

"You mean bribes?"

"I'm not saying that at all," Dobson disagreed. "I am saying the city leaders made it really easy for the railroad to place its new yards in Big Spring. And, as you know, Big Spring is the only place for miles with a readily available, year-round water supply. So, even though it might not look that way on the map, going via Big Spring makes sense."

"I guess I'll have to take your word on that, since I'm no railroad man," Jim replied. He looked warily out the window as the train slowed appreciably. He reached for the Winchester alongside his seat.

"What're we stoppin' for?"

"Water stop," Dobson explained. "We're just outside a little place named Cuthbert. We'll take on water here, then roll straight into Big Spring."

Keeping his rifle at the ready, Jim carefully scanned the gently rolling plains as the train came to a stop. Dobson stepped to the car's platform, watching as the fireman climbed the ladder to the rickety, wooden water tower's platform and swung the spout over the engine, where the engineer stood waiting to fill the locomotive's tank.

Suddenly, the fireman threw up his hands and toppled off the platform as the sound of a rifle shot echoed across the prairie. More shots rang out. The engineer crumpled to the top of the locomotive, then rolled off and plunged to the ground.

"Comanches!" Dobson shouted. He dove back inside and grabbed a Remington pistol, then smashed out a window with its barrel.

"Those sure ain't Comanches!" Jim hollered back. He had already levered his rifle, and took a quick shot at the oncoming riders who were topping a low rise.

"Blast it!" he exclaimed when his shot missed. A return bullet shattered the window, just above his head. "Chet, get this train movin'!" he shouted out the window. "We're sittin' ducks out here."

"Can't," Dobson yelled, as he fired at one of the horsemen. "They got the engineer and fireman. We're not goin' anywhere."

"Then we're gonna fight 'em off." Jim's comment was more of a growl to himself than a remark to Dobson. He grunted in satisfaction when his next shot took a raider in the shoulder. The man hunched over in his saddle and rode away from the fight.

A scream came from behind Jim. He whirled to see a trackman several seats away with an arrow in his chest. Clutching the arrow's shaft, the railroader staggered backwards, then slumped to the floor. Jim turned back to the window and resumed firing. A shot found its target and an outlaw howled as the slug tore through his belly. He drooped over his horse's neck, then jounced out of the saddle and slid to the dirt.

"We're outnumbered and outgunned," Dobson shouted. "We haven't got much of a chance."

Most of the unarmed railroaders huddled on the floor of the car. Bullets shattered windows and punched through the coach's thin wooden paneling.

"Long as we've got cartridges, we've got a chance," Jim retorted. He again took aim and pulled the trigger. His shot creased a mustang, sending the horse, screaming in pain and terror, into a frenzy of pitching and bucking. Its rider was thrown clear, landed hard, and rolled across the ground. When the renegade rode to his knees, Jim put a bullet through his side. Changing targets, the Ranger levered and fired, levered and fired, levered and fired. One rider pulled back, clutching a bloody shoulder, another fell backwards off his mount when smashed by one of Jim's bullets. Jim quickly jammed more shells into the rifle's magazine.

"You nailed that one for sure," Dobson

hollered. "Look. They're turnin' tail. Runnin' off."

Indeed, the raiders seemed to think the loss of three men to Jim's accurate Winchester and the shower of lead from other passengers made their attempt on the train more costly than it was worth. As Dobson said, they turned tail and ran.

"Let's make sure they keep runnin'," Jim said. He sent a few hurrying shots after the retreating outlaws. One slumped in his saddle when he took Jim's lead high in his back, but somehow managed to stay on his horse and ride off.

Jim took command. "Don't anybody move until we make sure they're not gonna regroup and return."

"I thought you said those weren't Indians, Ranger," Joshua Briggs said. His voice carried an accusation as he knelt by the dead trackman. "I'd say this arrow says otherwise."

"They weren't Indians," Jim said, calm and certain. "Except for a few bands of stragglers, the Comanches and Kiowas haven't been in these parts for years. Here, make yourself useful, Briggs."

Jim slid his Colt from its holster and passed it to Briggs. "If you see those *hombres* comin' back, use that gun!"

The Ranger stalked down the aisle. "C'mon, Chet, let's check on the others, then we'll see about those gunmen."

"Right, Jim."

Guns held at the ready, Jim and Dobson entered Reasoner's coach. Reasoner, who knelt at a bullet-shattered window with a short-barreled Smith and Wesson revolver in his hand, whipped around as they entered. His face was a mask of blood. When Jim's eyebrows shot up, he said, "Looks a lot worse than it is. I'm all right."

Sol Morris stood braced against the bulkhead. He held his left bicep with his right hand. Blood had leaked between his fingers, staining the shirt. Effie and George, the chef, huddled behind the counter.

"Mr. Reasoner, are you sure you're all right?" Dobson questioned.

Reasoner pulled a silk handkerchief from his pocket and wiped at the blood on his face. "It's only a bullet crease along my forehead," he said. "But I winged one of those Comanches, which made me feel a lot better. Don't worry about me, but Sol needs help."

"We've got to see to the men outside," Jim said. "Mr. Reasoner, you'll have to take care of the wounded on the train. There are a couple more hurt in the other car. Can you do that?"

"Certainly," Reasoner said, his mouth set in a firm line. He began reloading his pistol. "George, get some water boiling," he ordered. "Effie, I'll need all the clean cloths you have. Don't just sit there quaking. Get moving, woman."

With Reasoner taking charge inside, Jim and Dobson stepped off the train. First they checked the engineer and fireman on the off chance one of them was still alive.

"Sheesh. They never had a chance," Dobson sputtered.

The brakeman emerged from his hiding place behind a pile of rails on the first flatcar. Dobson hollered at him.

"Hey, Davis. Make yourself useful. Get someone to help you put Scully and Manning inside one of the cars. Then, get the tank filled on the engine, and steam built back up as fast as you can."

"I'll take care of it," the brakeman said, and scampered to the cars to find some help.

"Jim, I figure we'll want to get moving as quickly as possible, don't you?" Dobson said.

"Soon as I check those shooters. Then, give me a few minutes to see if I can pick up that horse I hit. It could give us a lead," Jim said. "Let's look at those bodies."

"You sure they're not Comanches, Jim?" Dobson asked as they approached the nearest body, which was laying face-down in the dry grass. "They sure looked like Indians to me."

Jim rolled the dead man onto his back. "Now what do you think, Chet?"

The so-called Comanche's dead blue eyes stared into the sun, and his black hair showed streaks of blonde, where sweat had washed away some of the dye.

"Well, I'll be a son of a . . . ," Dobson exclaimed.

Jim pointed at the hoofprints left by the raiders' horses.

"Unless they were herdin' a band of broncs they'd recently stolen from Texas ranchers, these weren't Comanche mounts. I've never yet seen an Indian ridin' a shod pony. A couple of those *hombres* were sittin' stock saddles, too."

He indicated the second body, which lay a few feet away.

"I also recognized that jasper. He's Tommy Vasquez, half-Mexican, half-Apache, and all bad. Last I knew, he was holed up somewhere down in the Big Bend territory."

"So, what's a half-breed owlhoot doin' way up here in north Texas?" Dobson asked.

"I'd say somebody hired him," Jim replied. He rolled over the last outlaw and whistled softly when he recognized him. "This sidewinder, Jake Foley, rode with Vasquez. Whoever wants the T&P out of business is hirin' some of the worst scum in Texas to get the job done."

Jim straightened up and searched the horizon.

"Chet, have a couple of the men load these bodies into one of the cars. I'm gonna get Sam, then see if I can locate that mustang, and mebbe get a lead on which way those gunmen headed.

Give me thirty minutes. If I'm not back by then, get this train rollin' without me. I'll catch up to you in Lamesa."

"All right," Dobson agreed.

Jim headed for the boxcar containing his horse. Sam whickered eagerly when the door opened and Jim clambered inside.

"Said you'd get a chance to stretch your legs," Jim said, and patted Sam's shoulder. Jim grunted when Sam buried his nose in his middle, then dropped his nose to Jim's hip pocket.

"All right, you can have a candy," Jim promised. "After you jump outta this car." Jim slipped the bridle over Sam's head and the bit into his mouth, then led him to the edge of the car. Sam hesitated for just a moment while Jim jumped, then the big gelding nimbly leapt off the train, snorting in excitement. Jim gave him the promised peppermint, then swung into the saddle.

"All right, pard. Let's see if we can come up with something." He put Sam into a trot.

A short while later Jim spotted the mustang he'd wounded. It was pulling at some bunch grass along the top of a nearby ridge.

"Let's round him up, Sam," Jim ordered. He dug his heels into the paint's ribs as he lifted his rope from the saddle horn and shook out a loop. When the bay mustang, startled, looked up and broke into a gallop, Jim pushed Sam into a dead run.

"Get him, Sam," he urged, as they raced across the plain. Once they came alongside the fleeing mustang, Jim skillfully made his cast, the loop settling over the bay's shoulders. Sam sat back on his haunches and dug in his hooves, bringing the bay to a sliding stop.

"Good work, pard," Jim praised. He jumped from the saddle. With Sam keeping the rope taut, Jim slowly approached the nervously snorting and pawing bay. He spoke softly to the horse. "Easy, boy, easy. It's all right. I just need to see how bad you're hurt. Let me have a look."

Reassured by Jim's calm voice and soothing manner, the mustang settled down and allowed Jim to examine his wound. Much to Jim's relief, his bullet had merely creased the bay's rump.

"You'll be all right, fella," Jim assured the horse. "I'll get some salve and fix you right up."

Jim took his canteen from the saddlehorn and dug a tin of ointment from his saddlebags. He washed out the blood-encrusted bullet slash, then coated it thickly with the salve.

"Looks like you'll have company the rest of the trip, Sam," he said with a grin, as he tied the bay's lead rope to his saddlehorn. "Now, let's see if we can figure out which way those renegades headed."

Jim swung back into his saddle, soon picking up the tracks of the fleeing outlaws' horses.

However, to his frustration, the trail soon disappeared on the rocky banks of a shallow stream.

"No tellin' which way they headed, Sam," he told his horse. "Might as well get back to the train."

He swung Sam back toward the tracks. The lonesome sound of the locomotive's whistle drifted across the plains. "Guess they're signallin' us," Jim said. "Better get movin'." He heeled Sam into a lope, which the mustang matched.

Chet Dobson waved when Jim topped the rise which overlooked the tracks.

"Figured we'd give you a warnin' before we rolled out of here," he explained when Jim reached the train. "Any luck?"

"Not much," Jim replied. "I did catch this horse, but the trail petered out by a creek over yonder. There's nothing more I can do here." He glanced at a small platform alongside the water tank.

"Who's runnin' the train?"

"Mr. Reasoner himself, along with the brakeman, Davis," Dobson answered.

"I'll need them to pull the boxcar alongside that platform, so I can get these horses loaded."

"I'll tell them."

"Thanks," Jim replied. "Soon as I can get the broncs on board, we can move out. I don't imagine those *hombres*'ll try again, but if they do, I don't figure we can hold 'em off a second time."

"We should be underway in ten minutes," Dobson said. "Just get those horses loaded."

Jim laughed. "You got it. Let's get outta here."

CHAPTER EIGHT

"Finally." Jim shoved his Stetson back on his head as he roused himself. "Didn't think we'd ever get here."

Chet Dobson, who was stretched over two seats across the aisle, sat up and rubbed the sleep from his eyes. "We in Lamesa?"

Jim watched the buildings glide slowly past his window. "Yep," he said. There had been a considerable delay at Big Spring while the bodies were taken to the undertaker, the wounded cared for by a local physician, and an engineer and fireman located to replace the bushwhacked trainmen. Now, at long last, the train pulled into its destination, with the sun already more than halfway along its descent toward the western horizon.

Jim spied his long-time comrade, Smoky McCue, waiting on the platform. "Looks like Smoky got my message. Chet, I'll meet up with you later," he said, when the train rolled to a halt. "I'll talk with Smoky and see how things stand here, then we can go over what needs to be done with Mr. Reasoner."

"That'll be fine, and it will also give me time to set up the guards for tonight," Dobson replied. "Tell you what. There's a decent restaurant here in town, Margarita's. Since it's just two blocks south of the station, Mr. Reasoner and I will be having supper there around eight, along with Bill Beedle, the superintendent on this job. So why don't you join us? I'll let Mr. Reasoner know."

"Sure," Jim agreed. "I'll see you then." He stepped onto the car's platform, then swung off the train.

Smoky McCue, a broad smile on his face, and one of his ever-present quirlies dangling from his lips, walked up and slapped Jim fondly on the back. "Lieutenant! It's been a while."

Jim returned Smoky's exuberant greeting with a light punch to his stomach. Smoky grunted. "Too long," Jim said. "And forget that 'Lieutenant' business. We've been trail pards too long for that."

"Sure, Jim," Smoky agreed. He took a puff from his cigarette. McCue was a sergeant, slightly shorter than average, but with a tough, wiry build. His black hair, shot through with gray, gave the illusion of a puff of smoke, hence his nickname. Deep gray eyes and a pencil-thin moustache looked a bit dandyish. His appearance had caused many a lawbreaker to underestimate him, much to their regret.

"Judging from your wire seems like you had a mite of trouble," he observed.

"Just a mite," Jim ruefully agreed. He started

for Sam's boxcar with Smoky a half-step behind. "Where are the rest of the boys?"

"Jeff's prowlin' around the camp here some-where," Smoky said. "Jorge and Kev are with one of the crews. You want to ride out there, or wait for 'em to roll back in?" He glanced up at the westering sun. "They'll be back in little more'n an hour, I'd say."

Jim thought for a moment and said, "I'd rather ride out there, but Sam needs a good feedin' and rubdown. I reckon things'll keep for that long. Let's head for camp. We can palaver as we ride. How far is it?"

Smoky laughed. "Expected that's what you'd say. The camp's less than half a mile from town. Sam'll be munchin' on oats in no time."

Jim's slid the boxcar's door open. Sam whinnied eagerly the moment he saw who it was. Jim climbed into the car and snapped lead ropes to the horse's halters. "I'll have both of you out of there in a jiffy," he said. "You'll get some rest tonight."

Sam pinned back his ears at Smoky when Jim led the horses out of the car.

"I see ol' Sam's as ornery as ever," Smoky said, laughing. "What's that you've got with him?"

"Outlaw's cayuse," Jim replied. He tied the bay's lead to his saddlehorn. "I shot his rider out of the saddle. Hoped I'd find a clue in the saddlebags or from the brand, but no luck."

"Looks like the horse got bit by a slug, too." Smoky ran his hand over the bullet burn along the gelding's rump.

"I did that," Jim said, as he slid the bridle over Sam's ears and the bit into his mouth. "Missed my first shot at the rider."

"Well, you patched him up all right. He'll be fine," Smoky tried to reassure Jim. He knew how much his fellow Ranger loved horses. Jim would be worried sick until he was sure that bay would recover. He'd often said he preferred equine company to that of most humans he'd met.

"Thanks, Smoke," Jim answered. He tightened Sam's cinch, then pulled himself into the saddle. "Where's your horse?"

"Soot's right out front," Smoky answered, walking alongside Jim when he heeled Sam into motion. Once again, Sam tried to nip Smoky. "That's enough, you," Jim said, slapping Sam on the shoulder. Sam snorted. When they rounded the corner of the rough-planked station, a charcoal gray gelding whickered a soft greeting.

"We're headin' out," Smoky assured the steel-dust with a pat to his nose. Smoky lifted his horse's reins from the hitchrail and climbed into the saddle. He turned Soot up the dusty street.

"How's Cindy Lou?" Jim asked, as the horses broke into a steady trot.

"She was doin' fine, last I saw of her," Smoky

replied wistfully, in response to Jim's query about the former dance hall girl, who was now Smoky's wife. "Just wish I could get home more often. You know how it is."

"I sure do," Jim said. "Don't know why our wives put up with us."

"Boy howdy, that's for certain," Smoky concurred. "Mebbe we'll get a nice, long leave when we're done up here. How's your family, by the way?"

"Julia's fine, and Charlie's growin' like a weed. As far as the leave is concerned, I wouldn't bet a hat on it," Jim answered, then quickly changed the subject.

"What about this new man you've got up here, Smith?"

"Kevin Smith," Smoky replied. "Nice young feller. Still a kid, kind of wet behind the ears, but he seems to have the makin's of a good Ranger. I think you'll like him."

"We'll see," Jim said. His gaze settled on a ramshackle building and corrals at the edge of town. "Ballard and Billings, Freighters" proclaimed the faded sign over the entrance.

"That one of the freight outfits the T&P is puttin' out of business?" he asked, jerking his thumb toward the establishment.

"One of them," Smoky confirmed. "I've already talked to the owners, if that's what you're gettin' at. I don't think they're behind anything."

"I'll want to talk with them anyway," Jim said. "This town got a marshal?"

"Yeah," Smoky answered. "Friendly cuss, name of Randy Erich. He appears to be a good enough *hombre* to handle any trouble in town, but of course that's as far as it goes. And of course his jurisdiction ends at the town limits."

Smoky pointed to a collection of tents and roughly constructed buildings that lined both sides of the newly-laid tracks.

"That's the camp. We'll be there in a few minutes. I'll introduce you around."

The two Rangers rode silently for the next few minutes. As they did, Jim studied the Texas and Pacific's construction camp, a conglomeration of temporary structures and tents, scattered around a few partially-built permanent buildings, which would service the trains once the new line was completed. The camp was nearly deserted, as most of the men were still out laying track. Those remaining glanced at the two riders, then ignored them.

Smoky indicated a walled tent at the far end of the camp. "That's where we bunk." He took a quick glance at the lowering sun. "You've got time to wash up before supper. Corral's just beyond the cook shack. You can turn Sam loose there. And here comes Jeff."

Smoky pointed out a rider approaching on a stocking-footed, blaze-faced buckskin. The rider waved his Stetson over his head in greeting when he spotted his fellow Rangers.

"Howdy, Lieutenant," Jeff Timmons called. "Heard you had a bit of excitement on your way over here."

"Just a bit," Jim said. "We'll talk about that later, when everybody's here. How you doin', kid?"

"Me and Socks are just fine, Lieutenant," the young Ranger answered, with a pat to his gelding's shoulder. Jeff had been with the Rangers for just over a year. Unruly brown hair showed from under his Stetson, and his brown eyes sparkled with the enthusiasm of youth.

"What're you doin' on horseback, Jeff?" Smoky said sharply. "You're supposed to be guardin' the camp today."

"Checkin' out that ridge yonder." Jeff pointed to a rise of land off to the northeast. "Thought I saw somethin' up there, so I went to make sure of it. Didn't find anyone, though. No sign of horses, neither. Must have been a mirage, or mebbe some antelope. Ground's too hard to leave any tracks."

"Good to see you're keeping a sharp eye out," Jim praised him.

"Thanks, Lieutenant," Jeff replied. "To be honest, I was kinda hopin' for some action. This has been one dull assignment so far. No sign of trouble at all."

"Well, with the railroad's payday tomorrow,

that bonus bein' handed out, and it bein' the Fourth besides, you're liable to get a bellyful of action," Smoky said. "Let's get the horses put away."

"Hold it, Smoke," Jim said. "How'd you know about that bonus? According to Reasoner, no one was supposed to know about it."

Smoky shrugged. "News like that has a way of wormin' out. Couple of the bosses get told, and next thing you know everyone's heard."

He chuckled grimly, and jerked a thumb toward the maroon and gold car being shunted onto a siding.

"Besides, that rolling palace ain't exactly inconspicuous. Everyone knows that's James Reasoner's car."

They reined up in front of the corral gate and dismounted.

"Once we're done here, with luck we can talk the cook out of some grub before the crews return," Smoky said.

"Well, we're gonna have to get a few things straightened out," Jim growled. He lifted the saddle and blanket from Sam's back, removed his bridle, and turned him into the corral.

After the horses were cared for, Jim deposited his bedroll and gear in the Rangers' tent, then the three men repaired to the mess tent, where they did indeed convince Hoskins, the old cook, to provide them an early supper.

"Food's not bad for a railroad camp," Jim said, as he shoved another piece of buffalo steak in his mouth. "I am curious about one thing, Smoky. Haven't seen any women or kids around here. Usually the families follow the track crews."

"Few weeks ago, orders came to send the women and kids back home," Smoky answered. "As Jeff said before, we haven't had any trouble yet, but that don't mean it's not comin'. Reckon the T&P'd rather be safe than sorry."

While they were downing final cups of coffee, the short blasts of a locomotive's whistle echoed across the camp.

"That'll be the crews headin' back for the night," Smoky noted. He gulped the last of his coffee. "Let's head on out there."

The Rangers pushed back from their table, left the mess and headed for the tracks. A wood-burning switch engine chugged slowly into camp, pushing three flatcars laden with track workers. Alongside the train two riders alertly scanned the surrounding terrain. Jim recognized Jorge Menendez, who was on his black, Diablo. The youngster on the other side of the train, riding a chunky bay, would be the new recruit, Kevin Smith.

Even before the train came to a complete stop, the workers began jumping from the cars. Some went toward the wash benches, but most headed straight for the mess tent. Jorge Menendez broke into a wide smile as he swung out of his saddle.

"Jim, howdy," he greeted his long-time riding partner. "Figured you'd have yourself a time before you got here. Good to see you again."

"You too, Jorge," Jim replied. "You been behavin' yourself? Keepin' away from the ladies?"

"Of course I've been behaving, but you know I'm irresistible to women," Jorge answered, grinning. He turned to the young man who now dismounted next to him. "Jim, you haven't met our new man. This is Kevin Smith. Everybody calls him Kev. Kev, Lieutenant Blawcyzk."

The rookie Ranger took Jim's hand with a firm grip. "Glad to finally meet you, Lieutenant. I've sure heard a lot about you."

Jim laughed. "Well, don't believe half of what these ornery ranahans tell you," he said. Jim liked what he saw, a hazel-eyed young man of eighteen or nineteen who seemed quietly confident and had no trouble meeting Jim's direct gaze. Tall and thin, almost lanky, Smith's auburn hair curled from under his broad-brimmed hat, and the Colt SAA on his hip seemed a natural fit.

"Glad to have you in the Rangers," Jim concluded.

"Thanks, Lieutenant, and I'll be sure to remember your advice about these other Rangers," Kevin replied.

Jeff shot a back-handed slap to Kevin's stomach.

"Ow! What'd you do that for, Jeff?" Kevin asked.

"Just to remind you that you're still the new man around here, and you'd better believe our stories, that's all," Jeff said, with a grin.

"That's enough horseplay for now," Jim said. "Jorge, once you take care of your horse, clean yourself up. Kevin, you wash up real good too," Jim ordered. "Then, both of you get enough chuck to tide you over for a while. I've got a supper meeting with Mr. Reasoner later on, and I want you two with me. Smoky, Jeff, you stay in camp, and keep your eyes peeled."

"You expectin' trouble?" Jeff asked.

"Always," Jim answered. "But especially right now, with a whole lot of cash sittin' just down the tracks. Jorge, Kev, we'll be ridin' out about seven-thirty."

"Okay, Lieutenant," Kevin said. "We'll be ready."

"Jim, you think mebbe we should post a guard outside Reasoner's car?" Jorge asked.

Jim rubbed his jaw thoughtfully before replying. "Reckon that wouldn't be a bad idea."

"What if Reasoner doesn't cotton to bein' wet-nursed?" Smoky questioned.

"That doesn't matter," Jim said. "Our orders are to make certain there's no more trouble for this

137

railroad, so what we say goes. Jeff, you'll take the first watch, until we get back from town. Kev and I'll take the next shift. Smoky, you get some shut-eye. You and Jorge'll have the last watch at Reasoner's car."

Later, as the three Rangers rode toward town and their supper with Reasoner and Dobson, Jim once again cast an appraising eye on Kevin Smith. He still liked what he saw. Well-mounted on the bay he called Brazos, Smith rode easily in the saddle, alert and watchful. He seemed to catch everything even the slightest bit questionable.

"Stop here for a minute," Jim ordered. He swung Sam to the rack in front of the town marshal's office, and dismounted. "I've got to introduce myself to the marshal."

Kevin and Jorge dismounted and followed.

"Can I help you gentlemen?" The man behind the desk dropped his newspaper and came to his feet. "Oh, howdy, Jorge, Kev," he said, when he recognized the Rangers. His gaze drifted to the silver star in silver circle badge pinned to Jim's vest. "I see you've brought a friend along."

Jim stuck out his hand. "I'm Lieutenant Jim Blawcyzk. Cap'n Trumbull ordered me here to take charge," he said.

The marshal's handshake was firm and honest. "Glad to meet you, Lieutenant," he said. "Randy Erich's my handle. I've got to say, I'm plumb glad you Rangers have been sent here. I'd be bitin' off more than I could chew tryin' to get to the bottom of all this trouble. I've got my hands more'n full just tryin' to keep these railroaders in line. Besides, I can't do anything about any trouble which happens past the town line."

Jim was favorably impressed by the marshal. Erich was a capable-looking man in his middle fifties, bald except for a fringe of gray hair, with pale blue eyes, and a face which looked quick to smile. But at the moment, Erich's friendly face carried a harried look, as if he had the weight of the entire world on his shoulders. As Smoky had said, Erich seemed to be a capable town marshal, but handling the problems connected with the arrival of the railroad was overwhelming his office.

"That's the reason we're here," Jim replied. "We'll handle the railroad's problems, and also help you in town as needed. In fact, that's why we came by. We're on our way to a meeting with James Reasoner and Chet Dobson. I'd like you to join us. It's a free meal, on the Texas and Pacific."

"I've never been one to pass up free grub," Erich replied. He took a narrow-brimmed hat from a peg and jammed it on his head. "Good thing I don't have to watch my grandkids tonight. I've got three, Rosalia, Brianna, and Angelo. They lost their dad in a wagon wreck awhile back, so I help my daughter with them, as much as I can." He retrieved his gun rig from its peg on the wall and buckled it around his waist.

"I suppose we'll be eating at Margarita's," he said.

"As a matter of fact, we are," Jim answered. "How'd you know that?"

"Not hard to figure out. Chet Dobson always eats at Margarita's whenever he's in town. You'll soon see why."

Erich slammed the door behind him and locked it. He got his horse from the corral out back, then he and the Rangers mounted and rode the few doors down the street to the restaurant. They left their mounts at the scarred rail out front, then Jim held the door open while the others entered.

The atmosphere inside Margarita's was redolent with the heady odors of chili peppers, spices, and frying meat. Jim squinted as he looked around the crowded, smoke-filled room, trying to locate Chet Dobson or James Reasoner. A buxom Mexican woman, wearing a low-cut red silk gown, approached.

"Jorge, *mi corazon*," she exclaimed. "I did not expect to see you this evening. And you brought my young friend Kevin along. Marshal, it's good to see you also. You are always welcome at Margarita's."

She turned her dark eyes on Jim, causing him to blush when she ran her frank gaze over his lean form.

"You must be Lieutenant Blawcyzk of the Rangers, no?" she asked. "I was told to expect you."

"Yes, I am," Jim admitted. "And the pleasure is all mine."

"I am Margarita. Mr. Reasoner and his party are waiting for you in a private room in back. Follow me, *por favor*."

Smiling, Margarita crooked a finger. Her hips swayed provocatively in that skin-tight gown as she led the four lawmen across the crowded dining room and into an elegantly appointed salon.

James Reasoner greeted Jim when he and the others entered.

"Lieutenant Blawcyzk, you're right on time. As I mentioned before, I appreciate that quality," James Reasoner greeted Jim, when he and the others entered. Reasoner was seated at a table already laden with bottles of liquor and various appetizers, fruits and cheeses. Chet Dobson and two other men, unknown to Jim, were also present. Alongside those were two extremely attractive women, dressed in low-cut satin gowns, which showed off their figures to perfection.

Reasoner continued. "I see you've brought some of your colleagues along. That's fine. Ranger Menendez, Ranger Smith, it's good to see the two of you again. You also, Marshal Erich," he added, nodding to the local lawman.

"Lieutenant," Reasoner went on, "Permit me to introduce William Beedle, the superintendent of construction for the new spur, and Joe Tate, who is, or I should say was, construction foreman. He's now our chief guard."

Jim shook hands with both men. Beedle was in his early forties, Jim would guess, his dark hair thinning, and the beginnings of a paunch pushed out his belt. Tate was about ten years younger, stocky and muscular. His dark eyes narrowed as he studied Jim.

"Also, I would be remiss if I didn't introduce their companions. These fine ladies are Dorothy Jackson and Patricia Fellows."

Both women gazed boldly at the Rangers. Dorothy was of Creole blood, dark-complexioned, tall and well-proportioned. She wore a shimmering sapphire-blue gown which complemented perfectly her dusky skin and shining dark eyes. Patricia was a redhead who wore a black gown that contrasted wonderfully with her fair skin, green eyes, and flaming red hair.

Once the introductions were completed, Reasoner invited, "Gentlemen, please, have a seat. Margarita will begin serving shortly. In the meantime, would any of you care for a smoke, or some whiskey?"

He waved toward a rosewood box in the center of the table.

"I have some of the finest Havana cigars here,

as well as Kentucky bourbon, Old Granddad's to be precise, from my own private stock. After our meal, I have a fine French brandy which I'm certain you'll enjoy. I have it brought in especially from New Orleans."

He lifted the humidor from the table, and held it out for Jim.

"Lieutenant?"

"No, thank you," Jim politely declined.

Jorge chortled. "You won't get the lieutenant here to drink anything stronger than sarsaparilla, nor smoke," Jorge explained. "Won't catch him cussin', either, nor with any women, 'ceptin' his own wife. Beggin' your pardon, ladies." Jorge smiled at Dorothy and Patricia. "Also, Jim says his prayers every night, and even goes to Mass on Sunday, whenever he's near a church. If more men were like him, there'd be a lot less trouble in this world. Which would put us Rangers out of business, I might add."

"Never thought I'd meet a Texas Ranger who's a regular choirboy," Marshal Erich observed.

"Oh, Jim sure ain't no choirboy," Jorge clarified. "Far from it. Any renegade he's tangled with can tell you that, at least them that can still talk. Quite a few of them have found that out, much to their regret. Most of 'em are in Boot Hill. Jim also loves a good game of poker."

Jorge reached for a cigar, a bottle of whiskey, and a glass.

"Far as myself, I for certain ain't no choirboy," he said, laughing. He poured himself a generous splash of Old Granddad's.

"Is that correct, Lieutenant?" Reasoner asked. "You don't imbibe?"

"No, I don't, but I'd purely appreciate some sarsaparilla if it's available."

"Certainly," Reasoner answered. "I'm sure Margarita will have some sent in."

"Of course. It will only take me a few moments to have your drink, Lieutenant," Margarita said.

Once Margarita left, Reasoner turned to Jim, a scowl on his face. "Lieutenant, Ranger Timmons is standing guard outside my private car. He told me you ordered him to do so."

"That's correct, Mr. Reasoner," Jim replied. "There will be Rangers on guard continually, until the bonus money is handed out tomorrow morning."

Reasoner protested. "There's really no need for that. Besides, Joe is in charge of security, and I have every confidence in him."

Jim's face took on hard planes that said he would not back down. "Mr. Reasoner. *You* asked for Ranger protection. You've got it. That means you'll fully cooperate with any decision I, or my men, make. Seems everyone in town knows about the bonus cash in your safe, despite what you told me. Thus, I will have one of my men on duty at all times. Do I make myself clear, sir?"

"Perfectly," Reasoner grudgingly agreed. He turned to his head of security. "How do you feel about that, Joe?"

"I'm much happier knowing the Rangers are on duty, Mr. Reasoner," Tate drawled. "I'm downright nervous about that money, what with everything that's happened on this job. I won't rest easy until it's distributed."

"I guess the matter is out of my hands, then," Reasoner conceded.

"I'm happy you agree," Jim stated. "While we're here, though, there are a few other things we need to discuss."

"And we shall," Reasoner said. The door opened, and Inez, one of the waitresses entered. She carried a tray holding bowls of soup and two bottles of sarsaparilla. "However, that can wait until after we enjoy our meal. There will be plenty of time for business later. Lieutenant, I sincerely hope that's a satisfactory vintage." He laughed, and passed Jim a sarsaparilla.

Jim was chafing with impatience by the time the lengthy meal was finally completed. The food had been delicious, far better than Jim's usual trail fare of bacon, beans, and biscuits, but plans needed settling and Jeff Timmons needed to be relieved. At last, after dinner drinks were served, and cigars lit.

Reasoner puffed on his cigar. "Now, Lieutenant, we can discuss your needs and concerns," he said.

"We need to do that in private, Mr. Reasoner," Jim replied, nodding toward Margarita. While Patricia and Dorothy had departed once the meal concluded, Margarita had spent the evening at Chet Dobson's side, and showed no inclination to leave. *Now I know what Randy meant when he said I'd know why Chet always eats here,* Jim thought. Not that he blamed the detective. While Margarita was in her late forties, by Jim's estimate, she was still an attractive woman, with jet-black hair, smooth olive skin, dark eyes, and a flashing smile.

Dobson bristled. "We can discuss anything freely in Margarita's presence."

"I have my own business to attend to," Margarita diplomatically stated. "Chet, *mi corazon*, I'll see you later. Gentlemen, good evening."

She kissed Dobson demurely on the cheek, rose and then left the room.

"Now, Lieutenant, if you would please continue," Reasoner said.

"Thank you," Jim responded. "I'd like to begin by reiterating that, if the Texas and Pacific is to continue receiving Ranger protection, all of your people will comply with any orders or requests I or my men make. If you feel you can't abide by those terms, please say so right now."

"I'll make sure all T&P people understand that," Reasoner promised.

"Fine. Next, Sergeant McCue has confirmed Joe Tate and his men have been doing a good job, working with him to prevent more trouble. I intend to leave things as they are for the time being. The Rangers already assigned here will continue to provide protection for your crews. Meanwhile, I will be conducting my investigation, to try and determine who is behind the attacks on your railroad. Along with that, I will assist Sergeant McCue in his duties, whenever possible."

"What can we do to help?" Reasoner asked.

"I was just coming to that," Jim said. "You've already agreed to provide the records I've requested, so we're all set on that. Now, I'd like Mr. Beedle to tell me about any location along the right of way where an ambush might be likely, or where it would be relatively easy to destroy trackage or equipment."

"That won't be difficult," Beedle said. "I can provide that information first thing in the morning."

"I'd imagine I'll be a mite busy tomorrow, what with it being the Fourth and all," Jim replied. "Why don't we plan on the next day?"

"Fine. About eight a.m.?"

"Seven would be better," Jim answered.

"Then seven it is," Beedle agreed.

"May I make a suggestion?" Reasoner said. "I'd like to have Sol Morris in on that meeting.

147

As chief surveyor, he should have some valuable suggestions."

"That would be fine, as long as he's up to it with that wound and all," Jim agreed.

"He'll be there," Reasoner promised. "Now, is there anything else?"

"A very important matter," Jim responded. "Either I, or one of my men, will be acting as your bodyguard tomorrow. That will continue until you return to Abilene."

"I'm afraid I've been remiss," Reasoner apologized. "I neglected to inform you I will be leaving Lamesa shortly after I distribute the bonus money. I must be back in Abilene early the next morning."

"What if someone tries to stop your train?"

"There will be no money on it, so I doubt any robbers will make the attempt."

"Yes, but you yourself could be a very valuable hostage, Mr. Reasoner," Jim pointed out.

Reasoner gave a harsh laugh. "Hardly. The Texas and Pacific has made it quite clear to all of its executives there will be no ransom paid in the event of a kidnapping. Therefore, my value as a hostage is exactly nil. You have no worries there, Lieutenant. So, before we adjourn, is there anything else?"

"I'm sure there must be," Jim answered. "However, it's been a long day, and I can't think of anything right now. It's also high time Kevin,

Jorge and I relieve Jeff. I can go over any further issues with Chet as they arise. Unless one of you gentlemen has any other concerns at this time, we'll call it a night."

"I do need to stay in town a bit longer," Reasoner said. "Do you have any objections, Lieutenant?"

"I'd prefer you return with us; however, if Marshal Erich is willing to act as your bodyguard and accompany you back to camp, that would be satisfactory," Jim said. "Marshal?"

"Sure, I can handle that, Lieutenant," Erich answered.

"Then everything's settled. Gentlemen, we'll see you in the morning."

"Howdy, Lieutenant. I was wonderin' when you fellas would show up," Jeff said, when Jim, Jorge, and Kevin rode up to the siding where Reasoner's car stood. Along with Jeff, two shotgun-wielding railroad guards stood at each end of the coach.

"Got away as fast as we could," Jim said. "Any sign of trouble?"

"Nah, none at all. Everything's real quiet," Jeff reported.

"Good. We're gonna turn the horses out, then be right back. You and Jorge turn in and get some shut-eye, both of you," Jim ordered. "It's gonna be a long day tomorrow. Jorge, I'll see you and Smoky back here at two."

"Jim, I was gonna ride back into town for a bit," Jorge protested. "I want to hit the Crystal Palace for a couple of drinks, and I promised Monique I'd meet her tonight."

"Monique?" Jim raised a knowing eyebrow. "You're in love again, Jorge?"

"Monique Van Leur," Kevin said, grinning, before Jorge could respond. "Half-Dutch, half-Texan, and all woman. At least that's what Jorge claims."

"It is a curse, my attraction for the ladies," Jorge moaned. "However, I must do what I can to make them happy."

"Well, Jorge, I'm afraid you'll have to make Monique happy some other night, because you're staying right here in camp tonight," Jim said.

"But, Jim . . ."

"That's an order, Jorge. I'll see you at two."

Realizing further protest was futile, Jorge climbed back onto Diablo. "All right, Lieutenant. Mebbe I can at least scare up a card game." With his back stiff and his shoulders braced back, he gigged the black into a trot and headed toward the corral.

"Jorge seems pretty upset," Kevin observed.

"Yeah, he's real mad," Jeff confirmed. "You can tell. He called the lieutenant 'Lieutenant', rather'n Jim."

Jim shrugged. "He'll get over it. Besides, in a week or two, he'll have forgotten all about this

150

Monique woman. At least now it's only Jorge I have to worry about. Smoky used to be just as bad for the ladies, until he met Cindy Lou." He heaved a big sigh."Let's get the horses put away."

"You want me to take your horse for you, Lieutenant?" Kevin asked. He reached for the reins only to have Sam pin back his ears and bare his teeth at the young Ranger.

"Not unless you want to lose a finger or two," Jim said.

"I forgot to warn you, Kev," Jeff apologized. "That horse of the lieutenant's is a one-man animal. He'd stomp you into the dirt before he'd let you touch him."

"Sam's not that bad Jeff," Jim objected. "Kev, he'll be fine once he gets to know you."

"Sure he will," Kevin answered, dubiously eyeing Jim's angrily snorting paint.

"Well, it doesn't matter right now anyway," Jim said. "Let's get them put away, so Jeff can get some rest. Jeff, we'll be right back, then you can hit your mattress."

"I ain't goin' anywhere."

Once Sam and Brazos were fed, rubbed down, and turned into the corral, Jim and Kevin returned to the siding. They nodded a silent greeting to the Texas and Pacific guards.

"She's all yours, Lieutenant," Jeff said with a grin when they walked up. "I'm gonna get some grub, then hit the sack."

"You do just that, Jeff," Jim said. "We'll see you in the morning. Good night."

"G'night, Lieutenant. G'night, Kev."

Jeff strode away, headed toward the mess tent, but his shoulders sagged from weariness and he didn't whistle as he usually did.

"Okay, Kev, let's settle in," Jim suggested. He sat back against the front steps of Reasoner's car, holding his Winchester across his knees. "Keep a sharp lookout."

"Sure will, Lieutenant," Kevin replied. He took up a position at the opposite end of the car.

The remainder of the night passed quietly, Jim and Kevin reporting no problems when Smoky and Jorge relieved them. At six in the morning, Jim had awakened and was shrugging into his shirt when Smoky and Jorge returned from their shift.

"All quiet?" he asked.

"Very," Smoky answered. He took out the makings and began rolling a quirly. "Reasoner and Dobson got back around three. They were the only *hombres* we saw all night. Once they turned in, it was as quiet as the proverbial tomb. That's why I didn't stay behind and send Jorge along to get Jeff and Kevin. Figured they could use the extra sleep, and for an hour or so the T&P guards can keep an eye on Reasoner. Hope you don't mind, Jim."

"Nah, reckon it'll be all right," Jim said, then

chuckled. "Far as quiet as a tomb, not sure that's a wise choice of words, considerin'." He stepped over to the bunks where Kevin and Jeff were sprawled, sound asleep.

"C'mon, you two, rise and shine," he ordered, then delivered a sharp kick under each man's cot.

"Huh . . . what . . . ?" Jeff mumbled.

"You heard me. Time to get up," Jim growled. "I reckon it's just about time for breakfast. After that, all we've got to do for the rest of the day is make certain nobody makes a try for that money until it's handed out. After that, we'll help keep a lid on things in town."

"Uh, not quite, Jim," Smoky half-whispered. "There might be just, um, one other, uh, small thing." He took a deep drag on his cigarette.

Jim stopped, his gunbelt half-buckled. "Whadd'ya mean by that, Smoke?"

"Well, you see, it's like this," Smoky answered. "Last night, before we took our watch, Jorge and me got into a poker game with some of the railroad men."

"Don't expect me to cover your losses, McCue," Jim snapped.

"It's not that at all," Smoky replied. "It seems there's gonna be a boxing match in town today, as part of the Fourth of July celebration. One of the railroaders, a man name of Red McGuire, is challengin' all comers. Well, some of the railroaders started braggin' that nobody could beat McGuire, especially no Texas Ranger. We couldn't let that pass. So, we told them you'd take on McGuire."

Jim exploded. "You *what?* Have you finally gone totally loco, Smoke?"

Jorge broke in. "Jim. Jim. it's not that big a deal. We saw this McGuire. You can take him, easy."

"You mean that *you* can take him, Jorge," Jim retorted. "I don't want any part of this harebrained scheme. Forget it."

"Jim, you can't back down," Smoky pleaded. "We've all got money ridin' on you."

"Kiss it goodbye, then."

"What about the honor of the Texas Rangers, Jim?" Jorge asked. "If you don't fight McGuire, we'll be a laughingstock. None of us will be able to show our faces anywhere around here."

"Jorge, you . . . dad blast it." Jim knew Jorge was right. His men had neatly trapped him into the match with Red McGuire. If he didn't fight, then the Rangers would no longer receive any respect from the rough and tumble railroaders.

"Why don't you or Smoky fight him?" he suggested.

" 'Cause you're the best man with his fists we've ever seen, and they wanted our best man to take on theirs," Jorge said.

"Menendez, I just might use these fists on you

154

instead," Jim answered. "All right, you've got me cornered. Guess I've got no choice."

"We knew you'd come through, Jim," Smoky said. "Don't worry. This McGuire's a pushover."

"That's exactly why I'm worried," Jim answered. "And you'd better be right, Smoke. Otherwise, you'll be *Private* McCue. Bet your hat on it."

By seven forty-five, every man of the Texas and Pacific crews was gathered in front of James Reasoner's private car. Jim and the other Rangers, carrying their Winchesters and ready for any sign of trouble, were posted around the car.

"You see anything at all that looks the least bit funny, shoot first and worry about the consequences later," Jim told his men.

"Don't fret, Jim. We'll handle any trouble," Smoky said.

At exactly eight, Reasoner stepped onto the rear platform, along with Theodore McGarry, the paymaster. Once they were seated at a small table, which was already in place, Chet Dobson emerged from the coach, carrying a canvas bag and large box, which he placed on the table in front of Reasoner.

Reasoner held up his hands. "Gentlemen, please, quiet. I realize you're impatient to start celebrating, so I won't make a long speech. I just want to thank you for keeping ahead of schedule, despite all the difficulties you have faced. Now, I am going to draw names at random. When each name is called, that man will step up here, and be given a fifty dollar bonus by Mr. McGarry."

The assembled workers gave a collective gasp. Fifty dollars was a small fortune. As they began to cheer, Reasoner stopped them once again.

"Please. Let me finish. I want you to enjoy today, celebrating your accomplishments and the birthday of our great country, the United States of America. All I ask in return is that you be ready to work again tomorrow morning. Now, without further ado . . ."

Reasoner reached into the box, pulled out a slip of paper, and called "Hendrick MacPherson."

The streets of Lamesa soon teemed with rail-roaders, all of whom had money in their pockets and were ready for a good time, prepared to blow off steam after weeks of dangerous, backbreaking labor. A few headed for the Post Office, which opened specially for a few hours, to send money home. Most, however, headed straight for the saloons and dance halls, ready to drink and gamble away their bonus dollars. Adding to the crowd were cowboys, ranchers, farmers, and their families, all in from the surrounding rangelands for a day of excitement. Small boys raced among the crowd, tossing lit firecrackers beneath horses' hooves, then dashing away before the indignant riders could get their mounts under control. And, in the center of Main Street, directly in front of the Golden Arrow Saloon, stood a makeshift boxing ring.

"It ain't gonna be easy keepin' this crowd in check," Randy Erich said as he met with the Rangers. "Already had to crack one jigger over the head with my pistol and lock him up. Sure glad you fellas are here."

"There shouldn't be too much trouble, other than the usual fights which happen with a crowd like this," Jim answered. "With us helpin' you keep an eye on things, we should keep any problems from gettin' out of hand. Folks are generally pretty friendly on a day like this."

"I hope you're right, Jim," Erich replied. He took a long pull on his quirly, then tossed the butt to the dirt and ground it out under his heel. "Lieutenant, I understand you're takin' on Red McGuire in the ring today."

"Not my choice," Jim answered. "I got railroaded into it."

Erich chuckled at the joke. "Well, I'll wish you luck. I'm gonna be refereein' the bout. I'll see it's a fair fight."

Jim sighed. "That's all I can ask. We'll see you later, Marshal. C'mon, men, let's get busy."

For the remainder of the morning, the Rangers patrolled the streets and alleyways of Lamesa.

As Jim predicted, there was little trouble. Most of that would occur later in the day, when men's tempers were inflamed by too much liquor. Now, however, except for a few minor arguments, easily quelled, the crowd was clearly enjoying the holiday.

Jeff pulled out his watch and glanced at it as he and Jim stepped out of the Crystal Palace Dance Hall and headed down Main Street toward the Golden Arrow. "It's just about quarter to twelve, Lieutenant," he pointed out.

"So, Jeff?"

"Fight's at noon. We're supposed to meet Smoky, Jorge, and Kev at the ring." Jeff couldn't suppress a grin. "You don't wanna be late."

"Jeff, if you're that eager, why don't *you* fight?"

"Uh-uh." Jeff shook his head emphatically. "I've seen Red McGuire."

"Whadd'ya mean?"

"Whoops. I wasn't supposed to say anything."

"Jeff . . ."

"Sorry, Lieutenant. I promised Smoky and Jorge. You'll find out soon enough anyway."

They continued their slow pace down the street. Two blocks later Smoky McCue came trotting up. "Jim, there you are. I've been lookin' for you. People're beginnin' to think you're not gonna show. Better hurry. McGuire's already there. Jorge and Kev are waitin'."

• • •

Jim and his partners approached the makeshift ring scratched out of the dirt of Main Street. Scrap timbers from the railroad marked the corners and supported the ropes. Michael "Red" McGuire, a huge Irishman, was already in the ring.

"C'mon, Ranger, I'm ready for you, I sure am," McGuire taunted when he spotted Jim. "Ain't no man has ever beaten Red McGuire in a fair fight yet. Sure, and you won't be the first, Texas Ranger or no."

At his first glimpse of his opponent, Jim paused for just a moment. Tall as Jim was, McGuire towered over him by a good four inches, and outweighed him by at least thirty pounds, not one of those pounds fat. Corded muscles stood out on the railroader's naked upper torso.

"If I live through this, I'm gonna kill you, McCue," Jim grimly promised. "You too, Menendez."

"Don't worry, pard. You can take him," Smoky replied.

"Mebbe with a sawed-off ten gauge," Jim growled.

"You've got no problem," Jorge tried to reassure Jim. "Don't forget, the bigger they are, the harder they fall."

"The bigger they are, the harder they *hit.* Bet your hat on that," Jim shot back. They pushed their way through the men and women surrounding the ring. Jim removed his Stetson, bandanna, gunbelt, and shirt, handed them to Jeff, and ducked into the ring.

The lively wagering got even livelier as the spectators studied the combatants. Noting the bullet and knife scars Jim's body bore, and that the Ranger was almost as hard-muscled as the railroad man, a few of them changed their wagers, but most stuck with their original choice, McGuire. The odds grew to ten to one against Jim, as just about every railroader placed his money on McGuire to handily win the bout.

Marshal Erich, acting as referee, waited in the center of the ring.

"Gentlemen, this will be a clean fight, and since it's my fight, I'll set the rules," he warned sternly. "Three minute rounds, no limit on the number. The fight will continue until one of you wins by a knockout, one quits, or I stop it. Shake hands, good luck to both of you, and come out fighting."

Jim and Red, glaring at each other, shook hands silently, then retreated to their respective corners.

At the clang of a borrowed locomotive bell, they stalked to the center of the ring, circling for a moment while each sized up his opponent. Red threw the first punch, a terrific overhand right. Jim ducked his head to the side, so the railroader's ham-like fist whizzed harmlessly over his shoulder. Then, he jackknifed in agony, as with deceptive speed for so large a man, Red sank his left fist deep into Jim's belly. The sledgehammer blow lifted Jim a foot off the ground, still doubled over Red's fist, then he staggered back to drape his arms over the ropes. Red drove several more punches into Jim's gut, then, at Erich's order, retreated to the center of the ring. Jim hung on the ropes, gasping, trying futilely to force air back into his tortured lungs.

Groggily, Jim came off the ropes. Knees rubbery and eyes blurred, he sought his opponent. He threw a right hook that bounced harmlessly off Red's ribs. A following left to the belly, delivered with all the power Jim had, barely caused Red to grunt. Red's next punch was a right uppercut which landed solidly on Jim's jaw. Jim sailed backwards and landed face-up halfway across the ring. He slid under the ropes and lay still, half-senseless.

"C'mon, Ranger, get up," Red taunted. "Where's that Ranger gumption I've heard so much about? Get back on your feet and fight, Mister!"

Jim's vision faded, his eyes refused to focus. Vaguely, as if from a great distance, he heard the shouts of the spectators and the strained voice of Smoky McCue urging him to rise. Dimly, he was aware of the rising and falling arm of Randy Erich as the marshal began the ten-count. When

161

Erich's voice echoed "seven", the clanging of the bell pierced through to Jim's fogged brain. Several pairs of hands dragged him to his corner and propped him against the post.

A bucket of cold water splashed over Jim's face and chest shocked him back to his senses.

"Jim, are you all right, pard?" Smoky asked. He sounded worried. "Mebbe we should throw in the towel."

"I started this, and I'm gonna finish it," Jim's voice was gritty, and he spit out a mouthful of blood. "Nobody's ever gonna call a Texas Ranger a quitter."

Jorge massaged Jim's shoulders. "You sure, Jim?"

"Positive," Jim replied. He pushed his partners away and came to his feet when the bell clanged for the next round.

"Gotta end this quick," Jim muttered, as he walked slowly toward Red. *He tags me solid again and it'll all be over.*

McGuire wore a confident grin as he stalked his foe.

Jim ducked under Red's first punch and landed a solid left to his stomach. Red grunted, more surprised than hurt, and air whooshed from his lungs. Jim sent three more blows slashing into the big railroader's belly before the startled Irishman could throw his next punch, which split the skin over Jim's right cheekbone. Jim stumbled back, blood trickling down his face.

A left hook caught Jim squarely in the chest, driving him back against the ropes. Jim bounced off, and began jabbing fast and hard at Red's eyes and face. He opened a cut over Red's left eye with a blow that staggered the big Irishman. Then, Jim's right fist crashed into his nose. Blood dribbled from both nostrils. Blinking to clear his vision from the blood flowing into his eye, Red swung wildly. He missed. Jim threw a left into Red's throat. The big man gagged, then stumbled as Jim drove his fists into the Irishman's face and body.

Desperately, Red battered down Jim's guard. He smashed a hard right to Jim's jaw that spun him around. Another vicious blow went to Jim's belly. He doubled up, then Red's left to the chin straightened him out. Jim's eyes seemed to be glazing over. Red drove in for the kill.

Red's final punch slid along the side of Jim's head as, with the last of his rapidly failing strength, Jim smashed his fist to the point of the big man's chin. Red's head snapped back from the force of the blow; he spun a half-circle, then toppled, landing face-down in the dust. He attempted to push himself back up, but, with a groan, collapsed to his belly. Jim slowly crumpled onto his side. He doubled up in pain, hands wrapped around his middle and gasping for breath. When he rolled onto his back, he grunted from the effort. He lifted his head, then it dropped back. Jim lay blood-covered and still, out cold.

Both men lay unmoving, oblivious to the frenzied shouts and curses of the spectators attempting to urge them to their feet. Then, with a low moan, Red pushed himself to his hands and knees and clambered to his feet. He staggered over to where Jim, now semi-conscious, struggled to rise.

"Here, Ranger. Let me help you," Red said. He grasped Jim's hand and pulled him upright.

"Thanks, Red," Jim gasped. They both ducked out of the ring and stumbled to a nearby horse trough. They doused their heads in the tepid water to soothe their cut and battered faces.

As the fighters sagged against the trough, chests heaving, one of the spectators loudly demanded, "But who won?"

"Yeah, who won?" Others in the crowd took up the chant.

"Red got up first, so he's the winner!" someone shouted.

"But he went down first, so that makes the Ranger the winner!" another person insisted.

"No, sir. Red won," yet another retorted. As the arguments grew louder, a full-scale brawl threatened to break out, until Red's deep voice sliced through the air, silencing the shouting mob.

"Listen to me, all of you," he ordered. "Nobody won. It was a draw, so nobody wins any money, but no one loses any, either."

He turned to Jim.

"Ranger, I never thought I'd see the day when another man could knock out Red McGuire, but you did, fair and square. You pack quite a punch."

Jim rubbed his swollen jaw. "You've got a pretty good wallop yourself, Red." He managed a grin, wincing with the pain.

"We'd make a hard team to beat in a saloon brawl," Red answered, laughing. "And if you ever need a hand, count on Red McGuire."

After they pulled themselves to their feet, Red continued, "Speaking of saloons, it's time we had a drink or two. He threw an arm around Jim's shoulders. "Let's get to the Golden Arrow. I'll buy the beers."

"It's a deal, as long as you make my beer a sarsaparilla," Jim replied.

"Sarsaparilla! That's a kid's drink," Red exclaimed. "What kind of a man drinks sarsaparilla?"

"The kind who just knocked a big Irish railroad man out cold," Jim said, chuckling. "Are we gonna have to fight again?"

"Not a chance, Ranger. Not a chance," Red answered. "My poor head couldn't take the pounding."

"Good, because neither could mine, not to

mention my guts," Jim agreed. He pressed a hand to his battered gut and grimaced. "Can't recollect my belly ever takin' such a beatin', so let's just get those drinks instead. Besides, it's the Fourth of July, and we've got some celebratin' to do."

Arms around each other's shoulders, walking shakily, Jim and Red headed for the Golden Arrow. Most of the spectators, still wrangling over who really won the bout, trailed close behind.

CHAPTER NINE

"Jim, you might not want to look at yourself in a mirror for a while, Smoky said with a chuckle as Jim settled stiffly onto his bunk in their tent. It was well after midnight, but Jim's face was still a swollen mass of cuts and bruises.

Kevin laughed. "Yeah, and I'll bet you won't be shavin' for quite a spell either, Lieutenant."

"You might want to keep in mind you're still on probation, Private," Jim growled in mock anger. He yawned. "Dunno about the rest of you, but I'm gonna get some sleep."

After a long day of keeping the Fourth of July celebrations from getting out of hand, breaking up fights, making arrests, and watching over the Texas and Pacific construction camp, Jim and the others were about to retire for the rest of the night. Joe Tate and his men were on guard duty until morning.

"Sounds like a fine idea to me, boys, especially since Jim there's gonna have us up and riding before the crack of dawn," Jorge agreed from his bunk, where he lay enjoying a last cigarillo. "*Buenos noches*, y'all."

Within minutes, the tent reverberated to the steady snores of five worn-out Rangers.

Jim woke in the pitch-black hours well before dawn. Still sore and restless, he decided to go for a walk in the cool night air. He slid into his denims and pulled on his socks. He was sitting on the edge of his bunk, getting ready to stomp into his boots, when a tremendous explosion knocked him flat on his face. A jagged shard of hot metal sliced through the tent's roof, skimmed over Jorge's bunk and buried itself under Jeff's cot. A thin spiral of smoke drifted toward the tent's ceiling.

"Wha—?" Smoky said from the ground, with an oath. The blast had knocked him clean off his mattress.

"Explosion. Hustle, men," Jim ordered. He pulled on his boots, scrambled to his feet and grabbed his gunbelt, then strapped it on and pushed open the tent flap.

Pandemonium greeted the Rangers as they rushed out of their tent. Flames leaped from the wreckage of the main storage warehouse. Smaller explosions rent the air. Jim grabbed a railroader by the shoulder as the man ran past, stopping him short.

"What happened?"

"One of the locomotives blew up," the railroader said. "It flattened the supply shed. We've gotta stop that fire from spreading, before it destroys the entire camp." He pulled from Jim's grasp and ran on toward the conflagration.

"Let's give 'em a hand," Jim shouted. He broke into a run with the rest of the Rangers at his heels. Already hoses were being attached to locomotives, so water could be pumped from the engines' tanks and trained on the wind-whipped flames. Jim and his men joined a line of railroaders who had formed a bucket brigade, scooping pails of water from the river alongside the tracks, passing them along hand over hand, and splashing the contents against the burning building.

Joe Tate rushed up. "Never mind the ware-house," he shouted. "It's too far gone. We've got to wet down the rest of them, before we lose the whole shebang."

Efficiently, he divided the men into groups, sending them to wet down the roofs and sides of the remaining structures, several of which were already smoldering from the intense heat of the burning supply warehouse.

The men fought a pitched, seemingly hopeless battle against the raging infernos. Finally, when the gray light of the false dawn streaked the eastern horizon, most of the flames had been doused and the main blaze beaten down to a few flickering embers. Weary men dampened down the remaining hot spots and checked the debris for possible victims.

Jim stood with Red McGuire near a still-burning mound that had been a small warehouse when another explosion sounded. A heavy blow slammed into his back. A white-hot poker sliced along his ribs. He arched in agony, staggered, and started to pitch forward into the flames.

"Hey, easy there, Ranger." Red McGuire grabbed Jim and jerked him back before he toppled into the blaze. "Wouldn't do to lose the only man who can stand up to me in a fistfight."

"Thanks. Much obliged, Red," Jim mumbled. He staggered again when he attempted to take a step. "What hit me?"

Red squinted at the blood-oozing tear in Jim's back. "Looks like a piece of metal, probably from whatever just blew up," he said. "You'd better get over to the infirmary."

"We've still got work to do," Jim insisted. "I'll go after we're done here."

"You sure?" Red studied Jim's eyes. "You don't look okay to me."

"I'm sure. Positive. I'm fine." Jim stumbled against Red.

"Jim, you're goin' to the infirmary right now," Red ordered. "No two-ways about it. Come on."

Jim took one faltering step and began to sag. "Mebbe you're right," he said.

Red grabbed Jim as he fell, lifted his two hundred pounds as easily as a sack of feathers and draped him over his shoulders.

"I am, Ranger," Red replied. "I am right, and you know it."

Jim said nothing.

Red carried Jim into the big infirmary tent. "Got another one for you, Doc." His voice boomed in the confines of the canvas-covered quarters. Several men were already inside, awaiting treatment.

Now conscious, Jim said. "I'm all right, Big Red. Put me down."

"Another medical expert who knows more than his doctor," muttered William Rosner, the railroad's physician. "Well, put him down, Red. Let him prove it."

"Sure, Doc." Red grinned. He stood Jim up and let him go. Jim swayed, barely able to stay upright. Beads of sweat broke out on his forehead.

"You still think you're all right, Mister?" Rosner said.

"Reckon mebbe you'd better look me over at that." Jim put a hand on Red's arm to steady himself.

"Now you're talking sense. Lie down on your stomach on that vacant table over there. I'll be with you as soon as I'm done with this man."

Rosner returned his attention to a gandy dancer with a broken arm.

Once Jim was stretched out on the table, Red said. "Jim, I'm gonna get back out there and help mop up. I'll check on you later."

"Fine, Red," Jim answered. "I'll see you in a bit." Jim laid his head on his arms, his senses whirling.

It seemed Jim had just dozed off when Doctor Rosner's voice gently broke through to his fogged brain.

"Sorry I had to wake you, but I'm about to start working on that wound in your back, Lieutenant Blawcyzk," Rosner apologized.

"Not . . . not a problem, Doc." Jim slurred his words. "Um, er, Doc? How'ju know me?"

"I watched your boxing match with Red McGuire," Rosner said. He lifted a blue bottle from a shelf over the table. "Just so you'll know, I had my money on Red." He held out the bottle to Jim. "You want a slug of this laudanum?"

"No thanks," Jim answered. "I've gotta keep my head clear."

"Suit yourself, although it's a bit too late for that," Rosner said. "Looking at what's left of your face after that fight, my diagnosis is the beating you took is the cause of your vertigo, not the wound in your back. Although that certainly didn't help you any." He took a clean strip of cloth from the shelf and knotted it.

"You might want to bite down on this, if the

pain gets too severe. And hold still while I'm poking around inside you."

He slid the cloth between Jim's teeth. Jim lay quietly while Rosner washed out the wound in his back, but winced in pain as he poured a carbolic solution into the tear.

"Now's when you might want to bite down on that cloth," Rosner advised. He lifted a probe from a pan of alcohol, then inserted it carefully into Jim's wound. Jim groaned, clamping his teeth down as a flaming sword seemed to be plunged deep into his back.

"Easy, Lieutenant," Rosner said in soothing tones. "I've got something here. I'll have it out in a minute."

Rosner twisted the probe once more, and deftly fished a battered chunk of metal out of Jim's back. He held it up to the lantern's light. "There, got it. You can relax for a moment. Then I'll stitch you up."

Rosner held the object he'd removed from Jim's back up to the light again, turning it slowly while he examined it.

"Hmpf," Rosner muttered. He continued to study the misshapen object.

"Somethin' funny, Doc?" Jim questioned.

"Sure seems to be," Rosner replied. "This looks like a bullet. I'd say you were shot, Lieutenant. I'd also say you were mighty lucky. The slug looks like it was pretty well spent by the time it struck you. It might've ricocheted off something first."

"You sure?"

"See for yourself." Rosner pressed the hunk of metal into Jim's hand. "What do you think?"

"You're right, Doc," Jim agreed. He recognized the battered chunk of lead for exactly what it was even though he didn't quite want to believe his own eyes. He hadn't heard a gunshot, but it was entirely possible the report had been muffled by the explosion he'd heard just as he was hit.

"I'm gonna hang on to this, Doc," he said.

"Fine with me. I don't need it."

"One other thing, Doc. Keep this under your hat," Jim requested. "Far as anyone besides you and me is concerned, I took a hunk of scrap metal tossed by that last explosion."

"Whatever you say, Lieutenant." Rosner eyed another man being assisted into the infirmary. One of his legs was twisted at an awkward angle.

"Put him down on that table," Rosner ordered. "I'll be with him in just a couple of minutes, as soon as I'm finished here."

He picked up a needle and surgical thread. "I'll have your back sewn up in a jiffy, Lieutenant. The slice along your ribs, too."

Rosner cleaned out the ragged wounds, washed out bits of flesh and dried blood, and stitched the edges together. "You'll need to take it easy for a few days," he advised. "You'll also be pretty sore. Are you certain I can't convince you to take some laudanum? It would help you sleep."

"No, Doc," Jim insisted. "I can't afford to have my senses dulled. And I'll be up and out of here as soon as it's light. I can't just lie around when there's a backshootin' drygulcher to track down."

Rosner started to speak, but Smoky McCue and Jeff Timmons rushed in and fairly ran to Jim's cot.

"Jim! Red McGuire told me you was hurt, real bad," Smoky said. "What happened? You gonna be okay?"

"A piece of metal caught me in the back. I'll be fine," Jim answered.

"He'll be fine if he listens to me, and rests," Doctor Rosner snapped. He was plastering a final strip of bandage to Jim's back.

"Just finish patchin' me up, Doc. Will ya?"

"Not until you promise me you'll spend at least the next two days in bed, Lieutenant. Minimum."

Jim shook his head. "I can't make that promise. Tell you what. I'll hit my bunk as soon as I find out why that engine exploded."

"You'll guarantee that?"

"Have I ever lied to you yet, Doc?" Jim asked, grinning.

"Get him out of here, as soon as I bind his ribs," Rosner growled at Smoky.

The doctor's attitude clearly worried Jeff. "Lieutenant, I'm not sure that's such a good idea," he said.

"Doesn't matter, Jeff," Jim said. "There's too much to be done."

"There's no point arguin' with him, Jeff," Smoky said. "I learned that a long time ago."

"Thanks, Smoke," Jim said. "Do me a favor, will you? Head back to our tent, and get my shirt and hat for me. I ran out of there so fast I left 'em behind."

"Sure, Jim. I'll bring 'em right here."

"Not here. Meet me at the corral. I have to make sure Sam's all right. Then, we can get to work."

Smoky chuckled. "I should've known. All right, we'll meet you at the corral. You just about finished with him, Doc?"

"Just about," Rosner replied. "Only have a couple more strips of bandages to get in place. After that, he can leave. However, Lieutenant, if you feel the slightest bit dizzy or nauseous, you get right back here."

"Deal, Doc," Jim said.

Through the smoke hanging over the construction camp, the rising sun looked blood red as Jim walked gingerly to the corral. He whistled sharply, and Sam detached himself from the rest of the nervously milling, snorting horses. The

176

big paint trotted up to the fence and nickered a greeting.

"Looks like you're all right, pard," Jim said, greatly relieved, when Sam stuck his head over the fence and shoved his muzzle against Jim's chest. "You just take it easy for a spell."

Jim gave Sam a peppermint, then turned when his name was shouted.

Red McGuire's voice boomed over the camp. "Jim! There you are! I couldn't believe it when I went to check on you and Doc Rosner told me you'd left. By me sainted mither, you're unbelievable. How ya feelin'?"

"Not bad. A couple hunks of hot metal in my back ain't nothin' after takin' a few punches from you, Red," Jim said, chuckling. "In fact, the doc told me that beatin' you gave me probably hurt me more than the metal."

"I could say the same thing," McGuire answered. His lopsided grin was evidence of the battering his face had taken from Jim's fists.

The jovial Red put on his serious face. "Are you sure you're all right, Mister tough Texas Ranger? Or are you lyin' to me?"

"I'm mending, Red, mending fine. Just waitin' for my pardners to show up. Red, do you happen to know how many men were hurt . . . or killed?"

"I'm not sure. Joe Tate's takin' a head count, so he should be able to tell you. I can't figure out why that locomotive exploded. The fires in all the engines were banked, what with no work goin' on over the holiday."

"Well, I'm fixin' to find out what exactly did happen," Jim responded. "Red, I'm no railroader, as you're well aware. I'd appreciate it if you'd tag along with me while I look around. Since you're a fireman as well as a trackman, you might spot something I'd miss."

"Be glad to, Jim," Red agreed. "Here comes your pards now. Looks like Joe's with them."

"Lieutenant, I'm sure happy to see you're up and around," Tate said when he got to the corral.

"That goes for all of us," Jorge added.

"Don't worry about me," Jim replied. "How about you fellas? Are all of you okay?"

"We're all fine," Smoky assured him. Along with Jim's shirt and hat, he held a tin mug. He passed the garments to Jim.

"Figured you might want some coffee, so I brought some along," he said. "Soon as you pull on those duds I'll give it to you."

"Much obliged, Smoke. Hot coffee'll go down good, bet a hat on it," Jim answered. He pulled on his shirt, tucked it into his pants, and jammed his Stetson on his head. Smoky passed him the mug, and he took a long gulp of coffee.

"Now I want to see the locomotive that exploded," he said. "From what Red tells me, there's no reason it should have blown up."

"Red's right," Tate confirmed. "Chet Dobson's

already over there, scourin' the ground. Mebbe he's found somethin'."

"Joe, did the blast cost you any men?" Jim asked as they started for the twisted remains of the locomotive.

"Not as many as I'd expected, Lieutenant," Tate said. "In fact, so far, only three: George Jacobs, the hostler in charge of readying the engines for the day's work, and Hi Jorgenson and Bob Slocum, the guards. I don't guess there's much left of 'em. We've got quite a few injured, though. Mostly scrapes and bruises, some burns, and a few broken bones. They should all be okay. The biggest problem, between the injuries and the damage, is the setback in construction. There's bound to be quite a delay until things are up and runnin' again. Bill Beedle is already working on that, trying to locate more supplies and find more men to replace those who got laid up. All right, that hole is where the engine was at. And there's Chet."

Chet Dobson peered into a deep crater. He looked up when the group approached.

"Joe," he said. "There you are. I was wondering where you'd gotten to."

"I heard Lieutenant Blawcyzk got hurt, so I went to check on his condition," Tate said. "You found anything yet?"

"Nah," Dobson said, shaking his head. "Quite a mess, though." He swept his arm toward the scene of devastation. In addition to the destroyed locomotive, three work engines had been blown off the tracks, and several others were damaged in varying degrees. Shattered cars, equipment, and supplies were strewn everywhere.

Almost as an afterthought he said, "Are you all right, Jim?"

"I sure am, and it sure is," Jim answered. "Looks to me like this was something more than just a boiler lettin' go."

"I don't reckon," Dobson replied. "Steam under pressure can cause a tremendous amount of damage."

"It sure can," Red McGuire confirmed. "Especially when someone does this." He plucked a cylindrical metal object from where it lay, half-buried in the dirt, and handed it to Dobson.

"That's a safety valve, isn't it, Chet?" Jim asked.

"It sure is," Dobson answered. "Dunno how I missed it. And someone took a hammer to it, jammed it so it wouldn't function right and release excess steam. That means the same someone, or an accomplice, also built up the engine's fire so steam pressure would go up until the boiler burst."

Tate didn't agree. "That's impossible!" he said. "First of all, how would they survive the blast? Second, no one could have gotten to that locomotive without bein' seen. Hi and Bob were two of my best men."

"Take a look for yourself, Joe." Dobson handed the valve to Tate, who quickly examined it. He swore under his breath when he was finished.

"I still don't see how they got by my guards," he insisted.

"Mebbe they didn't," Jim said.

"What's that supposed to mean, Ranger?" Tate's question was a snarl.

"Only that mebbe one of 'em rigged that engine to explode, then hightailed out of here. It'd be easy enough to pull off. You said 'they', Joe, but I'd be willin' to bet my hat it was only one man."

"But what about the others?" Dobson asked.

"It wouldn't be hard to put 'em out of the way," Jim answered.

"Or mebbe Jim's wrong. Mebbe more than one man was in on it," Jorge said.

Tate protested, loudly. "This is ridiculous. I'd stake my life on those boys."

Dobson held up his hands, palms toward Tate, and patted the air. "Take it easy, Joe. Simmer down a mite. Jim isn't accusing anybody, at least not yet. Isn't that so, Lieutenant?"

"For now, Chet, that's right," Jim answered. "When and if we find the bodies of those men, we'll know more. But right now, I wouldn't trust even James Reasoner himself."

"That's even more absurd," Dobson snapped. "Mr. Reasoner has been with the railroad for years. He'd have no reason to want the Texas and Pacific destroyed."

"Probably not," Jim agreed. "Still, he did leave for Abilene awful sudden like. It's pretty surprising that he didn't stay around for the holiday celebration, and his leaving turned out to be mighty convenient."

"I suppose at this point, you have to consider everyone a suspect," Dobson conceded.

"That's right. Even you and me, Chet." Jim grinned to take the sting out of his words. "Well, standin' around here yappin' isn't gonna help. Men, we're gonna turn this camp upside down. We need every bit of evidence we can find."

"Lieutenant, shouldn't you rest up some?" Jeff asked. "Red said you got hit pretty hard."

"I'll be fine," Jim insisted. "I can rest later."

After two hours of fruitless searching for evidence, Jim finally gave in to his wounds. He decided to head back to the Rangers' tent.

"Kev, you go with him, and make sure he lies down and stays down," Smoky ordered.

Jim grumbled. "There's no need for that, consarnit. Don't need wet nursin'."

"Lieutenant Blawcyzk, this time *we're* givin' the orders," Jorge said. "You look white as a fresh-washed sheet and you can't draw a deep breath. Kev, you heard Sergeant McCue give you orders, you do what he says."

"Right, Jorge," Kevin said, grinning. "C'mon, Lieutenant, let's get you back to your bunk. You need sleep, and lots of it."

Jim gave in. "All right. But, Ranger Smith, you get right back to work once I'm settled in. Y'hear?"

"Don't listen to him, Kev," Smoky said. "You stay with him. Make sure goes to bed and stays there. Hog tie him if you have to."

"All right, Sergeant."

Halfway back to the tent, Jim almost collapsed from fatigue. He draped an arm over Kevin's shoulders and leaned on the young Ranger the rest of the way. At the tent, Jim stumbled inside, then dropped face-down on his bunk. He didn't even realize that Kevin removed his boots and pulled a blanket over him. He slept soundly until the other men returned, just after sunset.

"Shh," Kevin said, "Jim's still sleepin'. You'll wake him up."

"I'm awake," Jim said. He rolled over and sat up on the edge of his mattress. He flinched when pain shot through his wounded back.

"You'd better lie back down, Jim," Smoky said.

"In a minute. Did you find anything?" Jim asked.

"Not enough to really mean anything," Smoky said. "We found some bits of clothing which may have belonged to one of the guards, and a few other odds and ends. But, really nothing of much help."

"Well, I'm gonna tell you something," Jim said. "But ya'll gotta keep it under your hats." Jim looked at each Ranger in turn, and they nodded their acceptance of his order. "I wasn't hit by flyin' scrap, leastwise not in the back. Somebody plugged me with a gun."

He reached into his hip pocket and pulled out the slug Doctor Rosner had dug out of his body. "The doc knows what happened, but he's promised to keep quiet."

Smoky whistled. He took the bullet from Jim, examined the battered piece of lead, and passed it to Jorge.

"First Abilene, and now here, Jim. Someone's tryin' awful hard to drygulch you."

"Or any one of us," Jim replied. "Someone could be after any Ranger he can down. Most likely, he's after all of us."

"Still, you've been his only target so far, Lieutenant," Jeff noted. "You'd best be careful. Real careful."

"We'd *all* best be careful," Kevin added.

Jim looked around at the faces of the Rangers in the tent. "Kev's right," he said. "So from now on, we work in pairs at all times. I don't want some bushwhackin' sidewinder to put a slug through any of you. Mebbe he'll think twice if

184

he has to take on two Rangers, rather'n just one."

"What about you, Jim?" Jorge questioned. "Looks like you're the main target."

"No drygulcher's gonna scare me off," Jim said. "I'm gonna track down the men we're after, or die a'tryin'. Speakin' of dyin', I'm dyin' of hunger. The cook tent still up?"

Smoky shook his head. "No, but Hoskins salvaged most of his equipment and he's managed to find enough supplies to make up some stew."

"Then let's grab some chuck."

CHAPTER TEN

Despite Jim's insistence he was not badly hurt, and while the shallow gash in his side was healing rapidly, the bullet wound in his back kept him laid up for several days. Still, he kept plugging away at his investigation as best he could while confined to his bunk. Enough human remains were found to identify the two guards and the engineer, so Jim eliminated them as possible instigators of the explosion. If they were the ones responsible, surely they would have given themselves ample time to get away before the locomotive blew itself to pieces.

Jim tried to reschedule his meeting with Bill Beedle for the day after the explosion, anxious to see the information he had requested about the terrain the rails would traverse. Instead, Beedle was occupied organizing the rebuilding of the shattered camp, ordering supplies to replace those destroyed, and attempting to get work on the tracks resumed as quickly as possible, so it was Sol Morris who poked his head into the Rangers' tent.

"Good morning, Lieutenant? May I come in?" Morris asked.

Jim looked up from the documents he was examining.

"Sure, come on in, but please, call me Jim."

"Of course. Bill sends his apologies. He's extremely busy trying to get things back in order. I hope you don't mind if I take his place," Morris explained. He winced slightly as he sat on the edge of Jim's bunk.

Jim noticed and asked, "That arm still botherin' you?"

"The arm? Not very much. I pulled a muscle fighting the fire, and it's stiffened up," Morris said. He looked at the bandages wrapped around Jim's ribs. Even at this early hour, the heat inside the tent was stifling, so Jim had removed his sweat-soaked shirt and tossed it on the bottom of his mattress.

"How about yourself?" Morris continued, "Looks like you took quite a beatin'."

"Feeling pretty good, actually," Jim answered. "This isn't as bad as it looks, just some torn up flesh. I've only got to take it easy for another day or two, while my blood builds back up. The doc'll take out the stitches by the end of the week."

"That's good news," Morris replied. "Now, let's get down to work. Let me answer any questions you have about the route."

He spread out a topographical map on Jeff's bunk.

"As you can see," Morris began, pointing to the map, "We have mostly level ground to cover, right from here to Twist."

His finger traced a squiggly line, which marked the right of way the Texas and Pacific tracks would follow.

"There are some rolling hills, none very high, about here, and there are several canyons, here, here, and here."

"I'll want extra guards posted at those sites," Jim said. "What about bridges and trestles?"

"Only a few. Most of those'll be short and quite low, as they'll mostly cross shallow dry washes. The only major crossings are here," Morris indicated a spot just north of Lamesa, "and here, where we have to cross a tributary of the Double Mountain Fork of the Brazos. That stream's not very deep, so the construction there hasn't given us much trouble."

"Are you saying the trestle is already in place, Sol?"

"Yes. All the trestles and bridges are done, except for some final work. It's more efficient to build the crossings ahead of time to keep from delaying the track crews."

"You've had no trouble at those spots?"

"Not really, just a couple of minor incidents, which were most likely mere accidents, not deliberate vandalism," Morris answered. "And since you Rangers arrived, there has been no more trouble at all. Don't know if that's mere coincidence, or if your presence has discouraged the troublemakers."

"How soon until the tracks reach those trestles?" Jim questioned.

"If it hadn't been for the explosion yesterday, we would have been crossing the first trestle later this week," Morris said. "Now, my best guess, if we can scrounge together the supplies we need, is the middle of next week."

"That quickly?" Jim asked. "Seems to me you could never begin rebuilding that fast."

"Jim, you don't know James Reasoner and Bill Beedle like I do," Morris differed, with a chuckle. "They'll move heaven and earth to get this mess cleaned up and construction started again."

"How about the Double Mountain Fork trestle? When will you reach there?"

"About a week after we finish laying track across that first trestle. Jim, I hate to leave you with any unanswered questions, but right now I really do need to get back to work. If you don't mind, I can leave this map. I'll get back as soon as I can to answer any other questions you might come up with."

"That'll be fine, Sol. You've been a great help," Jim said. "Yes, please leave the map. I want to study the route more thoroughly."

"Glad to oblige," Morris answered. "Anything to stop these attacks."

"We will stop 'em, bet a hat on it," Jim promised. "It's only a matter of time until whoever's behind all this slips up. I won't keep you any longer, Sol. *Muchas Gracias.*"

"You're welcome, Jim. If you need something answered right away, one of the men can always find me. I'll see you later."

"Later," Jim answered, already poring over the map.

Two days later, Kevin Smith stuck his head into the tent. "Mornin', Lieutenant," he said, with a smile. "Sleep well?"

Jim got up from his bunk. He yawned and stretched, then scratched his belly.

"Better'n I have the past couple of nights, Kev," he answered. "Pain finally didn't keep me awake half the night. Which reminds me, where have y'all been? Seems to me I haven't seen much of any of you around this tent, and all your bunks ain't been slept in. And what're you still doin' here, rather'n bein' where you should be, out lookin' for trouble? And what's that you've got?"

Kevin held his knife in his right hand and a circular metallic object in his left.

"First question, Doc Rosner said you needed as much quiet as you could get, so we unrolled our blankets outside so we wouldn't disturb you with our snorin' and tossin' around. Second question, Smoky, I mean Sergeant McCue, sent me back to keep an eye on you, just in case you had any fool notions about ridin' into town or somethin'," Kevin replied, with an embarrassed grin. "As far as what I was carvin' . . ."

He held up a silver Mexican five peso coin, which was roughly carved into a star surrounded by a circle.

"Thought I'd make me a badge like you fellas wear."

While Texas Rangers wore no official uniforms nor badges, it was becoming a custom for many of them, Jim and Smoky included, to commission badges carved from Mexican coins, or, as Kevin was doing, carve their own.

"You can forget what Sergeant McCue told you, and get back out there on patrol, *pronto*," Jim ordered. "Or else you'll never get to wear that badge. *Comprende*?"

"*Comprende*, Lieutenant," Kevin said. He slid his knife into its sheath and slipped the half-finished badge into his shirt pocket.

Jim dug in his saddlebags and pulled out a bar of yellow soap, his razor, tin shaving mug and brush, and a tattered towel.

"I'm gonna wash up and shave," he said. "You'd better not still be here when I get back."

"I'm gone, Lieutenant."

"Good. Tell Sergeant McCue I'm going to question those freighters like I planned. Also remind him I'm still ramroddin' this outfit, and he'd best not forget that."

"Yes, sir, Lieutenant. I'll do just that."

Kevin chuckled as he ducked out of the tent.

Jim's first stop in Lamesa was at the telegraph office, where he sent a long message to Ranger Headquarters, reporting what he had learned so far and asking if Captain Trumbull had any new information which might be helpful. After that, he went to see Randy Erich. The Lamesa marshal once again thanked him for the Rangers' assistance. However, he still was not able to think of anyone from town, nor the surrounding area, who might want to ruin the Texas and Pacific. However, he was able to provide Jim one valuable piece of information. The last of the farmers bought out by the T&P had just recently left for the New Mexico Territory. Erich agreed with Smoky McCue's assessment that none of the farmers or ranchers were in a position to fight the railroad and that most of them were satisfied with the price received for their lands.

After leaving the marshal's office, Jim mounted Sam and trotted over to the Ballard and Billings freight yard, where he draped his horse's reins over a tooth-scarred hitchrail.

"You stand here and behave yourself. I won't be long," he warned Sam, with a pat to his velvety muzzle. Jim pushed open the ramshackle building's front door and stepped into a cluttered, poorly lighted office.

A skinny clerk at the counter looked up with indifference, eyeing Jim from under his green eyeshade.

"Help you, Mister?" he asked.

"Is your boss around?" Jim responded, curtly. He had about as much interest in wasting time with this kid as the clerk seemed to have in speaking with him.

"Mr. Billings is on a run to Big Spring. Mr. Ballard is around here someplace, but he's busy."

"You reckon he'd be too busy to see me?"

Jim tapped the badge pinned to his vest.

The clerk took a deep breath. "I reckon mebbe not." He jerked a thumb toward the back door. "Last I knew he was out at the mule shed, so you should find him there. Big man, dark hair, long beard. You can't miss him."

"Much obliged," Jim said. He walked behind the counter, out the back door, and into the wagon yard. A string of curses from a long shed at the rear told him where he would find his quarry.

"Mr. Ballard?" he called.

A buckskin clad individual glared up from where he was rasping a mouse-colored mule's off rear hoof.

"Can't you see I'm a mite busy, Mister?" he grumbled.

"I won't take you from your work but a minute," Jim assured him. "Just got a few questions for you."

"Ranger, huh?" The muleskinner dropped the mule's hoof, then straightened up to stretch his cramped back muscles. "Well, it was time for a break, anyway."

With a slap on its rump, Ballard sent the mule trotting into its stall. He spat a long stream of tobacco into the dust. A few drops of brown juice dripped into his long, matted beard.

Jim offered his hand, and Ballard took it in a powerful grip.

"I'm Drew Ballard."

"Jim Blawcyzk."

"Blah . . . ?"

"Bluh-zhick." Jim, used to people stumbling over his tongue-twisting Polish surname, smiled. "Lots easier to go with plain ol' Jim, or Lieutenant, if you prefer."

Few Texans realized several large groups of Polish immigrants had been among the earliest settlers of the Lone Star State. Jim's ancestors were members of a band of Poles who had been recruited to work at a large cedar shingle mill, in the cattle town of Bandera, northwest of San Antonio. They had established permanent homes, and a church, St. Stanislaus, there.

"Jim works just fine," Ballard replied, with a shrug. "Now, state your business, so I can get back to mine."

"I just want to ask about your dealings with the Texas and Pacific."

"Not much to tell. The railroad's buildin' a new line which'll put me and my pardner out of business, leastwise around here."

"Around here?"

"Yep. Zeke Billings—he's my pardner, and the brains of the company—Zeke figures there are still plenty of chances for a jerkline outfit like ours. There's a new settlement startin' up further east, close to the state line. We're gonna set up shop over there, and haul goods in and out of the Indian Territories. So, you see, we've got no beef with the railroad, if that's what you're gettin' at. In fact, we'll probably make far more *dinero* than we ever did here."

Instinctively, Jim realized the tough old muleskinner was telling the truth. He grinned. "That's what I was gettin' at, all right." Ballard was the kind of man who would come straight at you, no holds barred.

"My pard told me you weren't holdin' a grudge against the T&P. I can see he was right," Jim said. "You think any of the other freighters might be tryin' to take on the railroad?"

"I doubt it," Ballard answered. "Matter of fact one of 'em, Frank Sells, hired on with the Texas and Pacific. He's workin' as a brakeman for 'em."

"How about the rest?"

"None of 'em are still around these parts, 'cept for Chuck Hardwin. The others all pulled out for New Mexico or Colorado."

"Where would I find Hardwin?"

Ballard spat once again before responding.

"Live Oak Cemetery, just past the church. Hardwin died four days ago. Apoplexy, from what the doc says."

"Sorry," Jim apologized. "I didn't know."

"Don't be," Ballard snapped. "Hardwin was an ornery cuss anyway. Not too many folks'll miss him."

"He got any kin?"

"Yep. A son, about your age. Kid hasn't been around for years. Even he couldn't get along with his old man. No, Jim, I'm afraid you're barkin' up the wrong tree if you think any of us freighters want trouble with the Texas and Pacific. We know we'd only be fightin' a losin' battle."

"I understand. Thanks for your time, Drew. Much obliged."

"Don't mention it," Ballard answered. "And, if on the off chance I should happen to think of anyone who might have it in for the railroad, I'll get word to you."

"Appreciate that," Jim replied. "Good luck in your new place. *Adios*."

"*Hasta la Vista*, Liuetenant. Sure hope you find the *hombres* you're after."

Jim headed back to where Sam was waiting. He glanced up at the sky as he picked up the reins, then climbed into the saddle.

"Looks like we're in for some rain, Sam,"

he told his paint. "But I've still got a few more places to visit before we head back. I'd better hunt you up a dry stall, pal."

With a storm coming on, Jim's next stop was the livery stable. As usual, he had to turn Sam into a stall himself because the hostler, afraid of Sam's teeth, refused to go near the bad-tempered paint. Sure enough, as Jim had sensed, the sky let loose with a cloudburst as he crossed the street to the Dawson County Courthouse. There, his Ranger credentials gained him swift and unquestioned access to the county land records.

Jim spent several hours poring over transactions between the Texas and Pacific and local landowners, but found nothing out of the ordinary. Finished, Jim headed to the Texas Café for a quick supper. After a slice of dried-apple pie and final cup of coffee, he went by the general store, where he purchased a new shirt and a supply of Sawyer's Deluxe Peppermints for Sam.

When he left the store, the sun poked through scudding clouds and the muddy streets had begun to dry. *Least the rain stopped. Learned all I can here in town, leastwise for now. Might as well head on back.*

When Jim rode back into the railroad camp, the first thing he noticed was Smoky pacing back and forth in front of the Rangers' tent. Seeing his grim expression, Jim knew something was dreadfully wrong. He kicked Sam into a gallop.

"Smoke, what happened?" he shouted as he pulled Sam to a crow-hopping halt.

"Jorge. And Kev," Smoky answered. "They were guardin' one of the track crews about ten miles north. They got ambushed. Kev downed two of the bushwhackers, but Jorge got creased. Took a bullet across his scalp. He's unconscious, but the doc says he should be okay. But three of the railroaders're dead. So are two more of the bushwhackin' skunks."

"What about Kev?" Jim asked.

Smoky shook his head, his face gloomy. "He took a rifle slug right through his belt buckle. He's not gonna make it."

Jim leapt out of the saddle and dropped Sam's reins to the ground.

"Where are they?"

"The infirmary," Smoky said. "Jim, you'd better hurry if you want to talk to Kev before he's gone."

Grim-faced, Jim followed Smoky across the camp and into the infirmary. Jorge lay on a bed, his forehead bandaged. Kevin was on the bed next to Jorge's. A blood-soaked cloth covered his abdomen. Jeff Timmons sat beside him. Tears streamed down his face.

Doctor Rosner caught Jim's eye and shook his head.

Jim softly called Kevin's name.

The young Ranger's eyes flickered open, and he gazed up at Jim.

"Lieutenant," he gasped. "Guess I . . . messed up."

"That's not what I heard, son," Jim said. "Smoke tells me you drilled a couple of those drygulchers plumb center. Nice shootin', kid."

"Thanks, Lieutenant." Kevin seemed to struggle for breath. "Never saw 'em comin'." His voice was almost a whisper.

"Don't worry about that," Jim said. "Just get some rest."

"How's Jorge?"

"He's gonna be fine. His head's too thick for a bullet to crack. You rest, like I told you."

"Gonna have plenty of time for that." Kevin shivered. His voice got even weaker. "Brazos. I want to see . . . Brazos . . . one more time."

"Sure, Kev. Of course."

Jim glanced at Smoky.

"I'll get him for you, Kev," Smoky whispered. "Be right back."

"Lieutenant . . . tell my folks . . . and my sis . . . I love 'em. Tell my kid brother . . . he's got . . . to be the . . . Ranger in the . . . family . . . now. Make sure he . . . gets my guns."

"I'll do that," Jim said. "I promise, Kevin."

"Yeah?" Kevin's answer was hardly louder than his breath.

Jim reached into Kevin's shirt pocket and

fished out the half-finished badge. He placed it on the dying young Ranger's breast.

"There's your badge, *Corporal* Smith. You're a man to ride the river with."

Jim stepped back and saluted.

"Thanks . . . Lieutenant," Kevin choked the words out. His voice was nearly gone and his breathing became even more labored.

Jim touched Jeff on the shoulder, and nodded at Kevin.

"Kev, we're gonna take you to Brazos now," Jeff told him, stifling a sob.

"Much obliged, Jeff. You've been . . . a . . . good pard."

When they started to lift Kevin from the bed, Doctor Rosner hurried over.

"What do you think you're doing?" he protested.

"Takin' Kev out to say goodbye to his horse," Jim answered. "You have any objections to that?"

Rosner withered under Jim's hard gaze.

"None. None at all."

"Good," Jim said. Gently, he and Jeff lifted their comrade from the bed, carried him outside, and placed him under a large cottonwood.

"Here comes Sergeant McCue with your cayuse," Jeff whispered. A moment later, Smoky led Brazos under the tree. The bay nuzzled Kevin's face and nickered softly.

"Brazos." Kevin managed to raise his hand to

stroke his horse's velvety muzzle. "You're a good . . . horse . . . pal."

Brazos blew softly into his friend's hand.

"Lieutenant."

"I'm right here, Kev."

"Please, make sure nothin' happens to . . . Brazos."

"I'll take care of him for you, son. You have my word," Jim promised. "He'll go home to my ranch and retire. He'll get fat and sassy, doin' nothin' but eatin' grass and dozin' in the sun all day long."

"And I'll hold Jim to that promise, pardner," Jeff added. He took Kevin's free hand in his.

"That's . . . good." Kevin tightened his grip on Jeff's hand, and he patted Brazos' nose.

"*Adios.*" Kevin shuddered. His eyes glazed, then he let out a long sigh and was still.

Jim laid a hand on Jeff's shoulder.

"He's gone, Jeff. But mark my words, we're gonna get the men who did this. That's a promise. And once we do, they'll wish that Satan himself had caught up to them first."

Jim, his blue eyes cold as ice, turned to Smoky.

"Get your horse. You too, Jeff. We're goin' after 'em."

"It's no use, Jim," Smoky replied. "Jeff and I rode out there, soon as we heard what had happened. That gully washer we had wiped out all sign. No telling which way to head."

"You sure, Smoke?"

"Sure as you're standin' there, Jim. Heck, you know I'd still be on their trail if there was any chance at all of runnin' them down."

"I know," Jim replied. His shoulders sagged. "Sorry, Smoke. Didn't mean anything by that."

"Don't worry about it," Smoky reassured him. "Soon as we get Kevin cared for, you might want to look over those *hombres* he downed."

Eyes moist, the three Rangers gently carried Kevin back into the small section set off in the infirmary as a mortuary. They laid him out, then stood with their hats off and heads bowed in silent prayer until Jim whispered, "Let's go, men."

"The bodies of those drygulchers are on a flatcar," Smoky explained. "I told Joe Tate not to move 'em until you had a look at 'em. He said either he or Chet Dobson'd stay with the train until you got back."

"Did you or Joe recognize them?"

"Nope." Smoky shook his head, then took a drag on his quirly. "But mebbe we'll get lucky, and you'll know who they were." He spotted the burly railroad detective slouching against the car. "Looks like Chet's waitin' on us. And he's got company." A tall man stood next to Dobson.

Dobson straightened up as the Rangers approached.

"Jim. Glad you're back," he said. "Have you seen Ranger Smith? How is he?"

"He didn't make it," Jim replied.

"I'm sorry," Dobson said. "Truly sorry. I liked that young man a lot."

Jeff swore. "When I catch up with the gut-shootin' coyotes who plugged him, they'll die real slow and painful, just like Kev did."

"Easy, Jeff." Jim soothed the grieving young Ranger. "We'll get 'em, sooner or later. Bet your hat on that. Chet, who's this with you?"

"Men, I'd like you to meet Andre Miller," Dobson introduced. "He's the foreman of the crew which was ambushed. Andre, Ranger Timmons, Sergeant McCue, and Lieutenant Blawcyzk."

"Andre. Pleased to meet you," Jim said. He flinched when Andre clasped his hand with a bone-crushing grip. Tall as Jim was, he had to look up to meet Miller's steady gaze. The foreman was a powerfully built black man in his mid-twenties. His broad back and muscular arms strained the shoulders of his faded blue work shirt. Miller could easily drive a spike with just one blow, and carry a keg of nails or heavy crosstie with ease. A bloody bandage was wrapped around his upper his left arm.

"Same here, Lieutenant," Miller replied.

"Jim's easier."

"Fine, then Jim it is. I'm sorry about your men."

"Thanks, Andre. Tell me what happened out there."

"Don't you want to have a look at these jiggers first, Jim?" Dobson suggested.

"They'll keep a little longer," Jim answered. "I'd rather get Andre's report of what happened while it's still fresh in his mind. Go on, Andre."

"Sure, Jim. We'd only been working for about an hour. There's some low hills where we left off yesterday. We'd had to make a shallow cut through those to lower the trackbed's grade. All of a sudden, this whole mess of shootin' started from the edge of the cut. One of the Rangers went down at the first shots. Two of my men were also cut down in that first volley."

Miller hesitated, his dark brown eyes blazing with anger.

"Keep goin', Andre," Jim urged.

"That young Ranger, Kevin, managed to drop two of the drygulchers before he got hit. I was able to drag him to cover, grab his rifle, and begin shootin' back. They killed another of my men and winged me before I hit two more of 'em. Guess that was enough for them, because they turned tail and ran. Sure wish I could've done more for the Rangers, but all I could do was hustle 'em back here to Doc Rosner quick as I could."

"You did good, Andre," Jim assured him. "In

fact, more'n most men would've done. I reckon you saved Ranger Menendez's life, and the lives of the rest of your men."

"I only wanted to stop those ambushers before they killed anyone else," Miller replied. "Didn't think about what I was doin' until after the shootin' stopped."

"Well, you did a good, real good. You wouldn't happen to recollect how many of those renegades got away?"

"I'd say no more than two or three, Jim. Good thing there weren't more of 'em, or they'd have wiped us all out."

"You're most likely right," Jim agreed. "Guess we might as well take a look at those bodies."

"Right, Jim."

Miller and Dobson climbed onto the flatcar and pulled off the canvas tarp covering the four dead bushwhackers.

Dobson let out a curse when he saw the bodies.

"Well, I'll be . . ."

"You know those men, Chet?" Jim asked.

"I sure do," Dobson said. "Well, two of 'em, anyway."

He pointed at one of the bodies.

"That there's Jasper Mitchell, and the one next to him is Lowy Burke. They both worked for the Texas and Pacific until a few months back. They got fired for slackin' on the job."

"How about the others?"

"No, I'm afraid not. Don't know 'em. Sorry."

"Well, I recognize one of 'em," Jim said. He indicated the body on the far end. "That's Bowie Purdue. I've run across him a few times."

"I recognize that name, Lieutenant," Jeff said. "Last thing I knew, he was servin' time in Huntsville for half-killin' a deputy marshal down in San Antone."

"He was," Jim answered. "Guess they must have turned him loose. Well, Huntsville won't be seein' him ever again."

The next morning, under a gloomy, gray sky, Texas Ranger Kevin Smith was laid to rest in the little cemetery next to the Lamesa Community Church. The local preacher did himself proud in commending the soul of the young Ranger, cut down in his prime, to the Lord.

Besides the Rangers, Marshal Erich, Chet Dobson and a number of the railroaders, along with a few people from town, attended the service. Jim and his men remained at Kevin's grave long after the rest of the congregation had departed. They watched in silence as the grave was filled in, and a rough wooden cross erected at its head.

"We'd best get back," Jim said reluctantly. "Need to see how Jorge's doin'."

"I guess you're right," Smoky agreed. "G'bye, kid," he murmured, looking at the fresh mound of earth covering the grave. "We'll ride the river together again someday."

"Yeah, we sure will, Kev," Jeff added, his voice breaking. "Pardner, I'm gonna miss you something fierce."

Jim dug in his vest pocket and fished out the half-finished badge he had removed from Kevin's chest before the service. Placing the badge atop the cross, "Rest easy, Ranger," was all he could say.

CHAPTER ELEVEN

After Kevin Smith's burial, the Rangers checked on Jorge, who had regained consciousness. However, he still suffered the aftereffects of the concussion the bullet crease had given him. Doc Rosner said he'd need several days to get back on his feet. Jeff, still deeply mourning the loss of his friend Kevin, was keeping Jorge company, along with a bottle of whiskey.

"Smoky, I'm still puzzled," Jim said.

"What do you mean, Jim?" Smoky looked up from his game of solitaire, and watched Jim pencil in a line along the route map Sol Morris left for him.

"Look here. Here's the most logical route for the Texas and Pacific to have chosen. It runs northwest from Abilene, not due west to Big Spring, then almost due north."

"So, what exactly are you gettin' at?"

"Just follow me for a minute, Smoke. Watch."

Jim traced another line on the map, this one from Sweetwater to Twist. Smoky frowned as he studied the two lines Jim had traced, then the heavier one that indicated the actual route the Texas and Pacific's surveyors had chosen.

"Jim, you're right. This doesn't make any sense! Why in the blue blazes did they build out of Big Spring? Either one of those other routes would have been more direct and far shorter."

"That's exactly the same question I've been askin' myself, Smoke, ever since I was handed this assignment. Chet Dobson told me the T&P chose this route because the terrain was lots easier to cross."

"Not that much easier to make such a round-about route worthwhile, I'd think." Smoky said.

"You're exactly right," Jim said. "Now, Chet also told me the town of Big Spring offered some mighty powerful incentives to be chosen as the starting point for this spur."

"An awful lot of *dinero* must've changed hands, to convince the T&P to take such a big detour."

"Right again, which is why I'm gonna take a ride into Big Spring," Jim replied.

"Why not take the train? Save you at least a day's hard ridin'," Smoky suggested.

"I've got a couple of reasons," Jim answered. "First, Chet told me he has to head back to Abilene tomorrow, so he'd be on the same train as me, and could figure out where I was headed. I'd like to have some time in Big Spring before anyone from the railroad realizes I'm there.

"Second, I'm gonna wire Cap'n Trumbull for some information, and I don't want to use the railroad's private telegraph line. There's a Western Union office in Big Spring. I can count on them to keep whatever I send confidential."

"You still think someone from the railroad's involved in all this?"

"I'm positive. Two of those drygulchers who killed Kev worked for the T&P in the past. One of 'em, Bowie Purdue, didn't care which direction his bullet went in from, front or back, long as he got well paid for his killin's. Mostly, though, some of what's happened could only be pulled off by someone who's got inside information. From where I stand, there's a railroader involved."

"Makes sense. How long you figure on bein' gone?"

"No longer'n I have to be," Jim said. "It depends on how quick I get a reply from Austin. I figure three, four days, tops. You're in charge until I get back."

"Don't have much choice," Smoky said. "What with you gone, Jorge laid up, and poor Kevin in the ground, there's just me and Jeff to handle things."

"You can ask Randy Erich for help if you need it," Jim replied. "And don't forget Joe Tate and his men."

"You've got somethin' else up your sleeve, Jim, don't you?"

"Could be. I'm figurin' whoever's been tryin' to put a bullet in my back is still here in this camp. With any luck, he'll see me ride out and follow me. Then there's the possibility he's in Big Spring. I want to give him a chance to try for me again. But this time, I'll be waitin' for him."

"That backshootin' son already *did* put a bullet in you, Jim," Smoky reminded him. "Next time, he just might plant one right plumb between your shoulder blades."

"In which case, you'll be in charge of this assignment permanent-like," Jim pointed out.

The tent flap opened. "Excuse me, but I'm searching for Ranger Jorge Menendez," the new arrival announced. "My name is Monique Van Leur."

Jim and Smoky scrambled to their feet and stared at the exquisite woman who had just stepped into their tent. Monique Van Leur was tall and statuesque, with flawless, dusky skin and wide brown eyes. A full bosom tested the bodice of her low cut, sapphire-hued dress.

"Beg pardon, ma'am," Smoky half-choked. "We didn't hear you coming. I'm Sergeant McCue, and this is Lieutenant Blawcyzk. But you can just call me plain ol' Smoky."

"How about I call you Sergeant McCute?" Monique answered.

She laughed.

Smoky blushed.

"I'm charmed to meet y'all," Monique fairly purred. She extended her hand. "However, 'ma'am' sounds so formal . . . and old. I would much prefer you simply call me 'Monique'."

"Beggin' your pardon once again, ma'am, I

211

mean Monique, but you could never be plain, and you're certainly not old," Smoky said.

"Why, thank you," Monique replied, her voice dripping with magnolia blossoms and mint juleps. "However, where is Jorge? I just found out he'd been hurt in a gun fight. I came to comfort him the moment I heard."

"He's in the infirmary, Monique," Smoky answered. "I can take you straight to him, that is, if the Lieutenant says it's all right."

Jim had been watching the exchange between Smoky and Monique with bemusement.

"Of course, Smoke," he agreed. "You go ahead. I'll see you before I turn in."

"Perhaps I can also see you before you turn in, Lieutenant," Monique hinted.

"I've had a very long day. I'm afraid I'll be sleepin' long before you return," Jim answered.

"It would be worth waiting up for me."

"I'm sure it would, Miss Van Leur," Jim agreed. "However, I have a wife and boy to consider. I'm a very happily married man. So is Sergeant 'McCute', by the way, in case I need to remind him of that."

"More's the pity," Monique pouted. "Well, at least Jorge will be glad to see me."

"I'm sure he will be," Jim said. "Good evening, Miss Van Leur."

"Good evening, Lieutenant."

Once Smoky and the woman stepped outside

into the gathering darkness, Jim chuckled. Monique Van Leur's "nursing" was sure to bring Jorge around . . . and fast.

Jim's Ranger star was hidden, snugged inside his shirt pocket, when, just after sunset the next day, he rode into Big Spring. Anyone seeing the lean, blonde rider mounted on the big paint gelding, both dust-coated and sweat-streaked after the hard run from Lamesa, would take him for just another drifting cowpuncher.

"Gonna find you a stall, then get myself a room," he said to Sam. "Can't do anything tonight, and havin' a real bed to sleep in for a change will feel mighty fine."

Sam tossed his head and snorted.

"And horse," Jim added. "Try to behave yourself with the hostler for once. I'm runnin' out of livery stables willin' to take you in. Now, there's a likely lookin' place over yonder."

Sam's response was a disgusted snort. He broke into a trot when Jim reined him down an alleyway toward the Horse's Haven Stable.

Once Sam was settled in, with the hostler having strict orders for his care as well as a warning not to get too close to the big paint, Jim obtained a room at the Spring House, the largest hotel in town. He washed up, then changed into a clean shirt and neckerchief. After having supper at a small café, he strolled around town, stretching his legs and taking in the sights.

Big Spring took its name from the huge natural spring in the middle of town. Thousands of gallons of clear, sweet water gushed forth from the artesian every day. It was the only reliable source of water for miles around, in any direction. Before the arrival of white settlers, it had been frequented by herds of wild mustangs, buffalo, and antelope. Roving bands of Comanches, Kiowas, and Shawnees also depended on it. Now, it was the hub of the thriving new town and was in fact the very reason for the town's existence. While Big Spring had been a bustling settlement for several years, the community planned for an influx of even more business as the new Texas and Pacific spur line neared completion.

After an hour or so, Jim walked over to the railroad station, then back up along Front Street, where he stopped at a quiet saloon. He drank a quick sarsaparilla before heading back to his hotel. Worn out, he said his evening prayers, undressed, and slid under the covers. Stretched out on a soft mattress, Jim was asleep the minute his head hit the pillow.

The next morning, Jim's first stop was the livery stable, to check on his horse. As usual, Sam had thoroughly terrorized the stable's hapless owner. After leaving the stable and having a leisurely breakfast, Jim's next stop was the Western Union office. There, he dictated a long message to Captain Trumbull at Ranger Headquarters. "This message is confidential, kid," he warned the clerk. "And you keep my identity under your hat, hear?"

"Sure, Lieutenant, I mean, Mister," the young operator agreed. "You gonna wait for the reply, or pick it up later?"

"I'll get it later," Jim answered. "You just remember, if anyone but me sees that message, it could cost you your job."

"Don't worry about me. I know how to keep quiet," the clerk assured him. "I'll lock the reply in the safe until you return."

After leaving the telegraph office, Jim headed over to the Howard County courthouse. As in Lamesa, his Ranger badge and credentials afforded him quick access to the land records. After obtaining the information he sought, Jim returned to the Western Union office.

"I'll be with you in a minute, cowboy, as soon as I'm finished with this gentleman," the clerk told him.

A cadaverously thin individual dressed in a checked suit and derby hat stood at the counter, tapping it impatiently with his fingers.

"I won't be very long," he assured Jim. "I represent Bendlak, Pella, and Grimes, a large St. Louis dry goods wholesaler. I am placing orders for several of my clients."

"Take your time," Jim said. "I'm in no hurry." He dropped into a chair and stretched out his legs as if getting ready to take a nap. Underneath his calm exterior, however, he was champing with impatience, hoping Captain Trumbull's reply to his wire had arrived.

After what seemed an interminable wait, the drummer concluded his business.

"Sorry, cowboy," he apologized.

"No problem at all." Jim's smile belied his anxiety. The minute the door slammed shut behind the drummer, he came to his feet.

"Your reply arrived a while ago, Lieutenant," the clerk said. "I'll get it."

He went to the safe, spun the combination dial, and opened it. He took out a yellow flimsy and handed it to Jim.

Jim quickly scanned the message.

"Do you need a reply sent?" the clerk asked.

"No, but thank you for pushin' my telegram through so quickly, and for keepin' quiet," Jim answered. He folded the message, slid it into his shirt pocket, and tossed the clerk a dime.

"Anytime, Lieu . . . I mean, Mister," the clerk said.

The door opened and another customer walked into the office. Jim turned away and stepped outside. He paused on the boardwalk, where he took the message from his pocket and read it again.

Will take day or so to obtain information requested STOP Special Courier will deliver package to you Big Spring soon as possible STOP Capt H Trumbull STOP

Jim tore the thin paper to shreds and deposited the remains in a half-full rain barrel.

He chuckled. *Well, Ranger, looks like you can lie around doin' nothin' but gettin' fat and lazy for a couple of days.* His gaze settled on a barbershop across the dusty street. "Now that's as good a place as any to get started," he said aloud. "A shave, haircut, and nice long, hot bath are just what the doctor ordered."

One reason Jim chose to stay at the Spring House was its location, directly opposite the Texas and Pacific depot. He could lounge on the hotel's awninged veranda in a tilted-back chair with his booted feet up on the rail and his Stetson tipped over his eyes. He could remain there, dozing, until the arrival of a train. At that point he would wander across to the station with the usual crowd of locals to see who was coming into town.

On the third day of veranda napping, Jim watched the westbound local from Dallas steam into the station. Among the passengers was a young woman, dressed in a conservative, dove gray traveling outfit. She caught Jim's eye as she stepped off the train and gave him a barely perceptible nod. Jim chuckled to himself as he touched the brim of his Stetson in a brief acknowledgement.

Figures Cap'n Trumbull's special messenger would be Pat. No one'd ever suspect her of workin' with the Texas Rangers.

Patricia Johnson was rather mysterious. She had arrived in Austin several years previously from somewhere back East, exactly where she never would reveal. Within a few months of her arrival, she had established one of the most exclusive "fancy houses" in the capital city. Her business had thrived, and with many of the local and state politicians, prominent businessmen, and even a few members of the clergy among her clients, she had no reason to fear being shut down. But that all changed the day a violent argument over one of her girls had led to the shooting death of an Austin city councilman. After the killing, the "better element" of the city demanded action, so Pat had been forced to close her establishment.

Pat subsequently met and married a handsome young Texas Ranger, who was gunned down in the line of duty a few years later. When her husband's killer was acquitted, she briefly returned to her former occupation, using all of her considerable wiles to lure the outlaw into a cleverly designed trap. What the murderer thought would be a night of passion ended when Pat pumped two bullets from a Derringer into his heart. Since no jury in Texas would ever have convicted the widow of a Ranger for avenging her husband's death, no charges were even filed against her. The proceeds from the sale of her business gave her a comfortable living, so she now divided her time between caring for her large home and gardens on the outskirts of Austin and working as a courier for the Rangers. Many times, when the Rangers needed a confidential and discreet messenger, Pat proved invaluable.

Jim watched appreciatively as Pat crossed the street and climbed the stairs to the Spring House. She was a beautiful woman in her late twenties, with short dark hair, wide green eyes, and a slim, well-formed figure.

Not long to wait now, he thought.

Jim spent the next two hours lounging in the lobby of the Spring House, ostensibly absorbed in reading week-old newspapers from Austin and Dallas. He barely glanced up when Pat, now dressed in a form-fitting red silk gown that perfectly complemented her emerald-hued eyes, descended the stairs and enter the hotel's dining room. After an adequate amount of time passed, Jim folded his newspaper and stepped into the restaurant. He chose a corner table, opposite Pat's.

When Pat's sherry arrived, she glanced over at Jim and smiled, lifting her glass in a brief greeting. Jim raised his cup of coffee in a return gesture. While he was working on his pecan pie, Pat paid her check and left, giving him a quick smile as she passed.

A moment later, screams came from the lobby. *Pat!* Jim dropped his fork, jumped to his feet, and raced into the lobby, where Pat struggled to escape the grasp of a tall cowboy, who gripped her left arm. Pat resisted. He attempted to pull her out the door.

Drunk, the cowboy pleaded. "Aw, c'mon, sister, I just want you to dance with me for a while, and mebbe later have a couple drinks."

"Take your filthy hands off of me!" Pat demanded.

"Aw, c'mon, just one little dance," the cowboy insisted. He staggered, but didn't let go.

Jim crossed the lobby in three long strides. He grabbed the cowboy by the shoulder and spun him around.

"I believe the lady said she wanted to be left alone," he said.

"This ain't none of your business, Mister," the cowboy snarled. He launched a vicious punch that caught Jim on the side of his mouth. Jim staggered back, and his boot heel caught in a seam of the Navajo rug in front of the desk. He fell backwards, hitting his head on the edge of the counter with an audible crack, then slumped to the floor.

"You . . . you beast!" Pat slapped the cowboy

sharply across his left cheek. "Get out of here, before I call the sheriff." The chagrined cowboy retreated. Pat knelt alongside Jim, who lay sprawled on the rug next to the counter. She pulled out a lace handkerchief and dabbed at the blood dribbling from the corner of his mouth.

"Mister, I'm truly grateful to you." Her voice quivered. "Are you badly hurt?"

"I don't think so, ma'am," Jim replied. He waggled his jaw. "Don't guess nothing's broke. This here blasted rug packed more of a punch than that *hombre* did. But my head's pretty thick. Seems like the only thing busted is my pride."

He chuckled.

"Nonetheless, I'm indebted to you. Here, let me help you up," Pat offered. She picked up Jim's Stetson and handed it to him, then supported him as he pushed himself shakily to his feet.

"Are you sure you're all right?"

"I'm just fine," Jim insisted. "Besides, I sure couldn't let that *hombre* paw you like that. Bet a hat on it."

"Still, you were very brave, and I'd like to thank you properly."

"There's nothing to thank me for, ma'am."

"Well, I happen to disagree. I'm sure you'll think of some way I can repay you."

Jim flushed deep red when Pat boldly ran her gaze up and down his lean frame. While he was not a handsome man, he did have rugged good looks, which many women found attractive. It always made him uncomfortable when one stared at him, as Pat was doing now.

"I think I'd better be on my way, ma'am," he said.

"I surely hope I'll see you again," Pat replied. "I'll be staying right here at this hotel for the next several days. You remember what I said."

"Yes, ma'am," Jim answered. "Right now, though, I'm just gonna get a drink or two, and hope they'll clear my head. Mebbe I'll run into you again."

"Make sure you do," Pat ordered. She turned and headed up the stairs, her hips swaying provocatively under that skin-tight gown.

Jim started for the door, then reversed course as if changing his mind. He walked up to the front desk.

"May I help you, sir?" the desk clerk inquired, peering at Jim over the spectacles perched on the end of his nose. The clerk had remained safely behind his desk throughout the entire incident, not making a move to assist Pat.

"You sure can," Jim said. "The lady who just went upstairs. Which room is she in?"

"You mean Miss Creamer?"

"That's the lady."

Once again, Jim was impressed by Pat's cleverness. She had checked into the Spring House under her maiden name.

"I'm afraid I can't divulge that, sir." The clerk sneered. "We run a respectable house here."

"Sure you do." Jim's voice dripped with sarcasm. "Just the same, I *would* like to make the lady's further acquaintance."

He took out a silver dollar and held it in his palm. The clerk shook his head. Jim then pulled a half-eagle from his pocket and spun it onto the counter top.

"Room Twelve," the clerk hissed, as he whisked the coin off the desk.

"Much obliged," Jim replied. "And I see you do run a respectable hotel. Most places I could have gotten her room number for that buck."

He turned on his heels before the clerk could muster a response.

Room Twelve was on the opposite end of the hotel from Jim's own. He hurried down the dimly lit corridor, then paused a moment to make sure the hallway was deserted. Once certain it was clear, he knocked softly on the door.

"Who is it?" Pat called.

"It's Jim," he answered.

"The door's unlocked. Come in," Pat said.

Jim pushed open the door, then jerked to a halt. Pat was sitting on the edge of her bed with a two-shot Derringer in her hand. The stubby, deadly gun was pointed straight at his stomach.

"Whoa. What's that for?"

"Sorry, Jim." Pat shrugged. She tucked the

snub-nosed little pistol into her beaded reticule. "A woman can't be too careful."

"You mean about some things," Jim retorted, grinning. "You've never struck me as the cautious type. And please, don't ever do that to me again. You scared me out of ten years of my life. How was your trip? Also, what in blue blazes is J.R. Huggins doin' in town?"

Jim had nearly shouted out Huggins' name in surprise, when he'd grabbed the "drunken cowboy" who accosted Pat, only to find himself confronting a fellow Texas Ranger.

Pat rose from the bed and kissed Jim gently on the cheek.

"And you've never struck me as the kind of man who scares easily," Pat shot back. "My trip? It was just fine, thank you very much. J.R. Huggins? Captain Trumbull felt you could use a man to take Kevin Smith's place. J.R. and I worked up that little scene on our way here. J.R. dropped off the train just before we got to town. We didn't want anyone to connect him to either of us. He'll be leaving for Lamesa on the regular supply train tonight, and will meet you there."

"You could've let me know. Sheesh."

"If you knew what was going on, our little act wouldn't have worked as well. This way you were completely surprised."

Pat tried, but failed, to suppress her laughter.

"Jim, you should have seen the look on your

face when you spun J.R. around and realized who he was. I hope he didn't hurt you too badly."

"Nah, the rug did most of the damage," Jim said, chuckling. "And I have to admit, you two put on a pretty good show."

He stood there, restlessly shifting weight from foot to foot.

"Aren't you going to at least remove your hat?" Pat asked.

"Won't be stayin' long enough for that," Jim said. "I just came for the package Cap'n Trumbull sent."

Pat dug into her floral-patterned carpet bag and removed a thick package and a manila folder.

"Do you mean these?"

"That's them," Jim said. He held out his hand and she gave him the folder.

"Aren't you going to read it?" she asked.

"I will, back in my room. Now, I'd better get goin'. It wouldn't be respectable for a lady travelin' alone to have a man in her room like this."

"Jim, since when have I worried about what people say?"

"Never, far as I recollect. That's one more thing I like about you, Patricia Johnson. Besides, you're far more of a lady than most of the society women I've run across."

"Thank you . . . I think," Pat said, smiling. "However here's something for you to think about. If you rush out of this room after only a few minutes, folks might start wondering why. It would be far better if you read those files right here."

"No one even saw me come to your room," Jim protested. "I made sure of that."

"The desk clerk knows, I'm certain. Desk clerks never miss a thing. And this is a small town. Word spreads quickly. Has anyone spotted you for a Ranger yet?"

"Don't think so."

"Then why chance it? Stay with me long enough so anyone who might know you came up here thinks we're doing what they're supposed to think we're doing."

"Huh?"

"Making love, silly."

"I dunno." Jim shook his head.

"Jim, you're too doggone stubborn. You know I'm right," Pat argued. "And you don't have to be scared of me. I realize you're happily married. Besides, Julia is one of the few women who have treated me decently. I wouldn't do anything to tempt you, or hurt her."

"I reckon that's so," Jim conceded. "Still, just being here with you is a temptation. But, I have to admit it'll be more pleasant spending an evening here with a beautiful woman, than tryin' to sleep in a stuffy tent full of sweaty, snorin' jaspers once I get back to Lamesa."

"Then it's settled," Pat declared, with finality. She handed him the package. "You'll remain here as long as it takes . . . all night, if necessary."

"It just might be that long," Jim said. He sighed when he opened the first package from Headquarters and removed its contents. "Lot more here to go over than I figured. Might as well get started."

He slid the first page from its file, and began to read. There were at least sixty pages of letters, files, and records to go over.

Three hours later, he dropped the last pages to the table.

"Jim, I can tell by the look on your face you've found what you were looking for," Pat said. "Am I right?"

His growing excitement had been apparent as he'd read through the documents.

"You sure are," Jim answered. He pushed back his chair, then yawned and stretched, flinching slightly when the still-healing wound in his back pulled. A smile of satisfaction played across his face. "It sure was, Pat. More than I'd ever expected, in fact. What's in here pretty much ties everything together."

"Then you'll have this whole matter wrapped up soon?"

"I dunno." Jim frowned, and ran his fingers through his damp hair.

"There's plenty here, all right, except the one final piece of evidence I need," he continued. Still can't pin this *hombre* down. I need to connect him to everything that's been pulled, and especially to Kevin Smith's killin'."

"You will, Jim, particularly because whoever he is, he's responsible for the death of that boy." Pat sounded as if she were certain. "You won't rest until Kevin's murderer, or murderers, are behind bars. As you're so fond of saying, I'd bet my hat on it. And I'm really fond of my hats, so there."

"Thanks, Pat. You know I can't tell you what is in those files, or whose names were mentioned."

"I realize that. I also know you'll be leaving before the sun's even up."

"How'd you figure that?"

Pat laughed. "I've been reading men for years. It's in your eyes, Jim."

Jim matched Pat's laugh. "Never could fool Julia, so why should I be able to fool you." He stood up and jammed his Stetson on his head.

"Guess I'd better try'n grab a couple hours shut-eye before I ride out. You catchin' the mornin' train to Dallas, then headin' for Austin?"

"I'm not quite sure," Pat answered. "Since I've got no special plans at the moment, I just might stay here in Big Spring for a while, and see what develops."

She smiled mischievously, with a devilish sparkle in her green eyes.

"Besides, I noticed a couple of cowboys out there who were mighty good-looking. I just might try and make their acquaintances."

"Sounds reasonable, and you're incorrigible," Jim replied. "You take care of yourself, Pat."

"And you be real careful, Jim. Don't you dare come home to Julia with any more holes in that handsome hide of yours."

"You mean besides the new ones I've already got? Don't hanker to," Jim replied. "However, now I've really got to get a move on."

He leaned down and kissed Pat lightly on the cheek.

"Good-bye, Pat."

"Good-bye, Jim. Now get out of here, before I start bawling."

"You'd be more likely to pull a gun and shoot me," Jim answered, grinning.

"That's enough out of you, Jim Blawcyzk," Pat retorted, then broke down laughing as Jim pulled the door open. After all, she had to admit he was probably right.

CHAPTER TWELVE

"Appears like we're ridin' into a storm, Sam," Jim told his horse. It was late afternoon, and they had pushed steadily northward since leaving Big Spring. The sky had been clear when they started out, just after sunrise, but, as the day progressed, its brilliant blue had been overtaken by a dull gray haze. The haze lowered and thickened into a solid overcast by noontime. In addition, the usually ceaseless north Texas wind had almost completely stopped, with only the faintest whisper of a breeze occasionally stirring the stagnant, oppressively humid air. Sweat made dark circles under Jim's arms and plastered his shirt to his chest and back. His hair was drenched under his hat, and his bandanna was also soaked from mopping his face and brow.

Sam snorted and tossed his head when lightning flickered on the horizon, and the rumble of distant thunder rolled across the prairie. His nostrils flared as he sensed the approaching storm, and he whickered nervously.

"You're right, pal," Jim said. "Sure seems like it's gonna be a whopper."

Jim reined Sam to a halt, then swung out of the saddle. He removed his hat and wiped sweat from the inside band. That done, he took his

230

canteen from the saddlehorn, uncorked it, and poured most of the contents into his Stetson. He allowed Sam to drink the contents. Jim took the last few swallows from the canteen for himself. Towering thunderheads were rapidly building on the northern horizon. It was time to take shelter, and fast.

"Pard, we'd better find someplace to ride this out. But first, I'd better make sure these papers don't get soaked and ruined."

Jim slung his canteen back over the horn, untied his slicker from behind the cantle and pulled on the yellow oilcloth. He then removed the files from Austin and a piece of oilcloth from his saddlebags. He wrapped the files in the waterproof cloth and tucked them back in the saddlebags.

Jim climbed back into the saddle. "C'mon, Sam, let's get movin'. That storm's comin' fast, and this is no place to be caught in the open."

Jim refused to put steel to a horse and therefore never wore spurs, but now he dug his boot heels a bit harder than usual into Sam's ribs. The startled gelding broke into a lope. Lightning flashed and thunder rumbled again, this time much closer.

The storm broke in all its fury before Jim found any shelter on the rolling, featureless plain. Buffeted by the wind, Jim pulled his Stetson lower on his head and hunched deeper into his saddle. Despite his slicker, wind-driven rain rolling off his broad-brimmed hat and down his collar soon had him soaked to the skin. Lightning struck all around, and the usually rock-steady Sam trembled nervously at each bolt. Rivulets of water ran off his drenched and steaming hide.

"Keep goin', bud," Jim urged his dejected paint, half-shouting to be heard above the storm. "We'll find a place to hole up somewhere. Until we do, we've got no choice but to keep movin'."

Doggedly, man and mount pressed on, through the howling, whirling wind, through streaks of lightning, and through drenching rain. Any thoughts of making Lamesa were soon abandoned. Jim's only desire at this point was to find shelter for the night. Someplace, anyplace where he and Sam could ride out the storm, then dry out after it abated. Finally, the rainfall slackened somewhat, and the sky seemed to brighten just a bit.

"Sam, looks like the storm's lettin' up a mite, anyway," Jim muttered. "Mebbe we'll find a place to make camp soon."

The terrain got progressively more rugged as they approached a series of low hills. With luck, they'd find an overhang to shield them from the elements. Just being able to get out of the wind would be a welcome break.

"Just ahead, Sam." Jim sighed in relief when a stroke of lightning revealed a low cliff that had several good-sized boulders scattered at its base. "We'll stop there for the night. We've stuck it out through worse, pard. You'll be . . ."

A bullet split the air alongside Jim's head, followed by the sharp crack of a rifle. He yanked the reins to haul Sam around.

"Get outta here fast, Sam. Can't see where those shots are comin' from. Give it all you got, horse!"

More bullets ripped through the air. Lightning flickered and the rifle spit again. Jim threw up his hands. He slewed out of the saddle. He landed hard, sprawled on his belly in the mud. Sam reared, galloped a hundred yards down the trail, then halted and turned back toward Jim. The big horse nickered in question at the prone, motionless form of his rider.

Jim lay stock-still, his face half buried in the muck. His left hand was clamped around his Colt, which he'd eased out of its holster and now held hidden under his slicker.

"Easy, Sam, stay back," he whispered to his paint, when Sam edged toward him, prancing anxiously. Sam stopped, his ears pricked forward as he eyed Jim.

Sure hope that hombre wants to make certain I'm done for. First time I've ever been happy about a lightnin' bolt.

That brief flash of lightning reflected off the

hidden gunman's rifle barrel and gave Jim the split second he needed to throw himself from the saddle before the bullet could find its target. As it was, the shots had come much too close for comfort.

Not daring to twitch a muscle, Jim listened hard for the sound of approaching footsteps over the noise of the storm, or retreating hoofbeats indicating the drygulcher had fled. He was taking a desperate chance the gunman wouldn't decide to put a finishing slug through him before leaving his cover. As the minutes ticked by, a cold sweat trickled down Jim's back, and his muscles tensed with the anticipation of hot lead tearing through his body.

Suddenly, Sam snorted. He jerked up his head when a slicker-clad figure materialized out of the mist, rifle in hand. The gunman glanced at Jim, then turned and headed for his horse. Sam whinnied a shrill warning. He danced away, ears pinned back and teeth bared.

"I'll take care of you," the gunman snarled. He raised his rifle and pointed it at Sam's chest.

"Hold it right there! You're covered, Mister!"

The gunman whipped around at Jim's shout and brought his rifle to bear. Jim rolled onto his side and fired once from under his slicker. His bullet smashed into the rifleman's chest. He spun halfway around, dropped his rifle, pitched onto his face, then rolled over. Jim leapt to his feet,

Colt at the ready. The gunman moaned in pain as he approached.

Jim recognized his bushwhacker. "Sol Morris!"

Morris choked. His voice was nearly a whisper. "Should've made sure of you first. Can't believe I was that stupid, fallin' for that old trick. Should've known you'd play possum. Suspected you'd had Austin do some diggin', and you were carryin' the evidence. Needed to see if the papers were in your saddlebags first. Most. Then what's in your pockets. You were a plain enough target. Figured I'd nailed you dead center. Would've gotten you, too, but . . . my side hadn't still bothered . . . me from . . . Abilene. Put my aim off . . . just a bit . . . reckon . . . that . . . made the difference."

The rain slackened to a drizzle, and in the distance the clouds began to break up as the storm blew itself out. The sun, now low in the western sky, lit up their bases. Jim hunkered beside the Texas and Pacific's surveyor. A large crimson stain spread rapidly across Morris' shirtfront. The pinkish froth bubbling from his lips indicated Jim's bullet had pierced one of his lungs.

"I knew it was someone workin' for the Texas and Pacific causin' all the trouble," Jim said. "Never imagined it was you, though. I figured it was Chet Dobson, 'specially after he left the camp. So, that was you tried for me back in Abilene."

"Sure was. I . . . heard you talking with . . . Reasoner. Knew right then you'd do . . . lot more digging . . . than the other . . . Rangers. Had . . . had to get rid of you. So, I waited in that alley. I . . . missed, but you . . . winged me. Then, in camp, after the explosion. Figured . . . I had you. Ranger, you've got . . . darndest . . . luck."

"You rigged that locomotive to explode," Jim flatly stated.

"Sure did," Morris gasped. He struggled for each breath. "It was . . . simple enough to . . . take care of the guards . . . and engineer. Nobody suspected me. I'd bet they didn't . . . even notice . . . I wasn't around . . . after I'd found out you'd . . . gone to Big . . . Big Spring, and came after you. It wasn't . . . unusual for me as . . . chief surveyor to be gone . . . days at a time. Took . . . train . . . to get to town . . . ahead of you. Watched to see . . . what you were . . . up to. I'd learned . . . practically every inch of . . . this area while locating the best . . . right of way. Once I was certain you . . . were heading back to the camp, I took a short . . . shortcut . . . Waited for you. Thought I'd laid . . . perfect . . . ambush. Bet you'd like to know . . . how I knew you went to . . . Big Spring."

"Simple," Jim replied. "You knew I'd left Lamesa, and since I hadn't headed north, Big Spring was the only logical choice. I'm surprised you didn't try for me in town."

"I was . . . going to, but that . . . woman was with you. Couldn't chance it. Better . . . if I killed you . . . out here, anyway. No one would know . . . what happened. You'd have just . . . disappeared."

"Morris, you don't have long," Jim said. Morris's breathing was becoming more rapid and shallow, and a rattle was developing deep in his chest. "Why don't you make a clean breast of it? I know who you were workin' for. It's all in those papers I got from Austin."

"Uh-uh, Ranger." Morris shuddered. "The Texas and Pacific is going to be ruined, whether . . . or . . . not . . . I'm alive. Not you or . . . anyone else . . . can stop . . . it."

"Morris, too many innocent people have died already. You don't want more deaths on your conscience, do you?"

"Don't matter . . . long as the railroad . . . suffers. You're wondering why . . . Reasoner wasn't . . . killed, aren't you? He . . . he would have been . . . in good . . . time. Wanted him to see . . . what happened to his . . . precious . . . railroad . . . first. That's why we planned . . . robberies, wrecks . . . all of it."

Morris convulsed and moaned. "Hurts . . . somethin' awful. Like my . . . chest's . . . on fire."

"But why?" Jim asked.

"You seem to have . . . figured out all . . . of that already . . . Lieutenant. But you'll never . . .

237

be able to . . . prove anything . . . against . . . you'll never . . . never . . . stop . . . plans . . . already in . . . place."

"Morris!" Jim shook the surveyor, but his words faded to an incomprehensible mumble. With a final, choking gasp, Morris stiffened and died.

Jim stared in frustration at the dead railroader.

He shook his head. "Morris was right," he muttered. "I was runnin' a bluff, hopin' I'd convince him to tell me somethin'. I've got the name I need from those files, but not one shred of proof tyin' that *hombre* to the robberies and killin's. And just what exactly are those plans Morris kept talkin' about?"

The rain had almost completely stopped. Jim pulled off his hat and shook the water from it. "Only shows what greed can do to a man."

Jim put his hat back on. Sam came up and nuzzled his shoulder. He nickered softly, then dropped his nose to Jim's hip pocket.

"I'm all right, Sam," Jim assured his horse. He dug a peppermint from his pocket and let Sam lip it off his upraised palm. "Seems like you are, too. And Morris? He's dead. He got exactly what he deserved for tryin' to shoot you, pard."

Jim patted Sam's nose. Sam nuzzled his cheek, then buried his muzzle in Jim's belly. Jim grunted.

"I reckon you're right, horse," Jim said. "We've got to get movin'."

To his surprise, the storm had passed, and the setting sun was gilding the clouds orange and gold. He hadn't even noticed the rain stopping, concentrating as he was on Morris during the surveyor's last moments.

"Good thing the rain's over," Jim murmured, as he looked at the hole his Colt had blasted through his slicker. "This thing's shot . . . in more ways than one. There's no way it'd keep me dry if it starts rainin' again, bet a hat on that."

Sam placed his nose in the middle of Jim's back and shoved hard.

"All right, all right. I get the hint, Sam. Dunno what your hurry is. We can't make town tonight anyway. I'll bury this *hombre*, then we'll ride as far as we can before full dark."

Jim took off his slicker and laid it across his saddle. Sam turned and once again nuzzled insistently at his hip pocket.

"Sure," Jim said, grinning. "You can have one more peppermint, pal. I reckon you've earned it."

No matter what, that horse always made him feel better. Sam could cheer him up out of his darkest moods. He gave Sam his candy, then removed his bridle and loosened the cinches, so the horse could graze more comfortably.

Jim dragged Sol Morris over to the base of a low cutbank. There he caved in the loose, sandy soil over the surveyor's remains, then piled rocks on the shallow grave to foil any scavengers. That chore completed, he retrieved Sam, then located Morris' horse, which was hidden in a small tangle of brush. He stripped the gear from the bay mare, which bore the brand of a Big Spring livery stable. With a quick slap on the rump, he sent the horse trotting toward town. It would find its way home without trouble.

"Need to buy some time. Don't want anyone to find out what's happened to Morris, at least not quite yet, anyway. It'll take that horse a day or two to get home. Hopefully that'll be enough," he told Sam, as he climbed into the saddle. "Mebbe once all is said and done, someone'll want to come back, dig him up, and plant him proper. I should've just left him for the buzzards, but nobody deserves that, not even a sidewinder like him. Well, let's get goin', horse."

Jim slapped the reins against Sam's neck, starting him into a trot.

CHAPTER THIRTEEN

Jim chuckled softly when he rode up the main street of Lamesa late the next afternoon, and spotted Jorge's black gelding tied to a hitchrail in front of the Crystal Palace Dance Hall.

"I guess Jorge's feelin' better, Sam," he said. "Bet he's with that Monique woman." He reined his paint in alongside Jorge's horse, dismounted, and tossed Sam's reins over the rail.

"I won't be long," Jim said. "Only the time it takes to roust Jorge outta there."

He ducked under the rail and headed into the dance hall.

At this hour, there was very little action in the Crystal Palace. Four painted women, sipping watered-down whiskey, lounged in a corner of the room. A few couples danced to the ragged music of a fiddle, guitar, and banjo. Once Jim's eyes adjusted to the dim light, he spotted Jorge, who was at a far corner table. As he'd expected, Monique Van Leur was perched on Jorge's lap.

"Jorge!" Jim called.

Jorge looked up, startled. "Jim, I didn't see you come in. "When'd you get back?"

"Pretty obvious you didn't," Jim answered, "and I just rode into town. I'm sure glad to see you're up and around again."

"That's thanks to Monique here," Jorge said. He took a puff on an evil-smelling cheroot. "She stayed with me nearly every minute."

Jim touched the brim of his Stetson in salute to the dance hall girl.

"I thank you for that, Miss Van Leur," he said. "However, I'm afraid Ranger Menendez must return to duty. Immediately."

"Must you always be so formal, Lieutenant?" Monique questioned.

"Not always. It depends on the circumstances," Jim explained.

"Jim, I was on guard duty all night," Jorge protested. "Can't whatever this is about wait?"

"No," Jim replied. "So finish your drink and meet me out front in five minutes. I'll go by the telegraph office, then we'll head out."

"Guess I might as well leave right now, then," Jorge grumbled. He picked up his glass and downed its remaining contents, then kissed Monique full on the lips.

"Sorry, darlin'," he apologized. "Mebbe we can get together tomorrow night."

"I'll be waiting for you." Monique rose from Jorge's lap. "That's a promise."

"I'll get him back to you as soon as I can," Jim said. He laughed to himself when he saw Monique scan the room for potential clients. Her wait would certainly not be a lonely one.

"Okay, Jim, what exactly's goin' on?" Jorge

asked the moment they got outside. "Must be real important, if you dragged me away from an afternoon with a beautiful woman."

"It is, but you'll have to wait until we get back to camp, so I'll only have to tell the story once," Jim replied. "Anything happen while I was gone?"

"Not much," Jorge answered. "Things have been real quiet. No sign of any trouble at all . . . which means it's comin', unless I miss my guess. Oh, yeah, there is one thing. J.R. Huggins showed up yesterday. Cap'n Trumbull sent him to take Kev's place."

Jim suppressed a smile.

"Sergeant Huggins is a good man, and one mighty tough *hombre*. I'm glad to have him with us."

Jim had worked with the rugged Huggins on several previous occasions.

When they got to the construction camp, Jim was amazed at the changes which had taken place while he'd been away. Almost all of the debris had been cleared, the destroyed tracks relaid, and the derailed switch engines were back on the rails. The frame of a new warehouse was already in place.

Guess Morris wasn't jokin' when he said Reasoner and Beedle'd waste no time gettin' things rollin' again.

"I'm gonna put Sam up," he said to Jorge.

243

"While I'm doin' that, I'd appreciate it if you'd round up the rest of the men. There's a lot I've got to tell y'all."

"Sure, Jim. Huggins and Jeff are out with one of the crews. Smoky's around here somewhere. I'll have 'em all back within twenty minutes."

Jorge rode off, whistling.

"Fine. I'll meet you at our tent," Jim called after him.

"Howdy, Jim," J. R. Huggins said as he ducked into the tent. "Sure hope I didn't hurt you. I didn't mean to hit you so hard."

Tall and lean, Huggins wore a white Stetson, pulled low to shade his brown eyes, and his brown hair, almost the same shade as his eyes, showed gray at the temples. Huggins was in his late thirties, but his face, tanned and weather-beaten from years of exposure to the harsh Texas sun and wind, made him look older.

"Nope, and it wasn't your fault," Jim answered, with a laugh. He rubbed the lump Huggins' fist had raised on his jaw. "That doggone rug is what did me in. Gave me a good crack on my skull when I hit the desk. I've gotta admit, I never expected to see you here."

"That was the idea," J. R. said. "Seems to have worked."

"Sure did," Jim agreed. "No one figured you and Pat were workin' together, or that you're a

Ranger, at least as far as I can tell. How's Cora and the kids?"

"Just fine, Jim," J. R. said. "I trust Julia and Charlie are doin' all right?"

"Sure are. And Charlie's growin' like a weed."

Smoky broke in. "Hold on here, just one dang minute. Jim, you already knew J. R. was here?"

"I did," Jim said. "To keep it short, Cap'n Trumbull sent me some files from Austin. Pat Johnson brought them to Big Spring, on the same train as J.R. On the way, the two of 'em cooked up a cute scheme so no one'd get suspicious about me and Pat meetin'. Far more important, however, is the information the captain sent. I don't need to tell you what you're about to learn can't leave this tent. Y'all might as well make yourselves comfortable, while I tell you what we're up against. Jeff, open the flap so we can see anyone comin'. Don't want any eavesdroppers listenin' in."

While the others settled on their bunks, Smoky and Jorge rolled and lighted quirlies. Jim dug in his saddlebags and pulled out the oilcloth wrapped files. After unwrapping the contents, he passed them to Smoky.

"First thing. A man died tryin' to drygulch me, so he could get his hands on those papers," Jim began. "Pass 'em around, Smoke. Lot to read, so just take a quick glance at 'em."

"What? Someone tried to plug you again?" Jeff said.

"Not just someone," Jim answered. "Sol Morris."

"Morris, the chief surveyor?" Smoky asked. He shook his head in disbelief.

"Yep. Morris was also the *hombre* who tried for me in Abilene, and put the slug in my back here. He won't be tryin' that again. Make sure to keep that under your hats. I don't want that news spread, at least not quite yet. As far as the Texas and Pacific is concerned, Morris is out checkin' the right of way. Read those papers, then I'll explain what I've figured out so far."

For the next hour the tent was silent, while the Rangers skimmed through the documents. Cigarette smoke formed a blue haze as Smoky and Jorge rolled and smoked several more.

"You're right, Jim, there sure is a lot to go over," Jeff said. "And readin' never was my strong suit."

"Mine, neither," Jorge said. "Can't make heads nor tails of some of this."

"Just keep on pluggin' at it," Jim said. "It's important."

Finally, Jeff Timmons finished reading the last file. He leaned back against his pillow.

"Lieutenant, this is dynamite stuff," he said. "Like you said, it sure seems to tie in with everything that's been happenin'. Big problem, though, is how can we prove it?"

"Yeah, Jim," J. R. agreed. "All these papers show is that the party in question tried to make a quick killin' by grabbin' up all the land along the right of way, before word got out."

"I know," Jim conceded. "That's the dilemma. We've got to come up with some proof. I tried to get Morris to talk before he died, but couldn't. All he'd say was that the Texas and Pacific was gonna be ruined, no matter what, and that nothing or no one, not even us Rangers, could stop that from happening. He mentioned something about 'plans', but I've got no idea what he meant."

"So what's our next step?" Smoky asked.

"I've got a couple of ideas," Jim replied. "First, I'm gonna see if Morris kept any other papers around. Schemers like these men usually don't trust each other, so he might've held onto somethin' we can use. You know where he bunked, Smoke?"

"He had a room at the Grande Hotel, Room 14, as a matter of fact. I met him there once," Smoky answered.

"Good, I'll check that room out," Jim said. "I've already sent a wire to Chet Dobson, warnin' him that somethin' might happen. Those plans Morris talked about could be for anywhere on the entire Texas and Pacific system, not just this line. I wired Cap'n Trumbull, too, and asked if he could spare any men to help Dobson out. Plus, we'll have Joe Tate tighten up security around here."

"What about us, Jim?" Jorge asked.

"All of you are to keep on doin' exactly what you've been doin', only be more careful than ever. I don't need to remind you a couple of those skunks who had a hand in Kev's murder are still out there. I don't want to lose another man to a bullet in the guts."

"Or to a slug in the back, like you got, Jim," Smoky pointed out.

"You're right, Smoke. Next step is we're all gonna ride into Lamesa tonight. I'll tell Joe Tate I'm givin' you the night off, just in case he's part of any of this. If he is, he'll most likely try'n pull somethin' while we're in town. We'll all head for the Golden Arrow. After a while, J. R. and I will take a walk over to the Grande. J. R., you'll keep a lookout, while I get into Morris' room and do some snoopin' around. Rest of you will act like you're enjoyin' a trip to town, but keep your eyes open. Any questions?"

The only response was silence.

"Seems like nothing anyone can think of, Lieutenant," Jeff said.

J.R. spoke up. "I've got a question," he said. "I need a horse. I took the train here, so mine's back in Austin."

"That's not a problem," Jim replied. "There's

a bay mustang in the corral. I downed his rider awhile back. You can use him."

"What about Kev's horse?" Jeff asked. "Seems to me Brazos'd be a better mount if we get in a runnin' gun battle."

"I promised Kev I'd take care of his horse . . ." Jim paused and rubbed his jaw thoughtfully. "But, y'know, I believe he'd be proud to know J. R. was ridin' Brazos. There's a nice chunky bay that belonged to Kevin Smith. J. R. He's yours now. Any more questions?"

More silence.

"Seems not," Smoky said after a moment.

"Good. We'll ride for town about seven-thirty."

From his bunk, Jorge began to softly sing *The Cowboy's Lament*.

"As I walked out in the streets of Lamesa, as I walked out in Lamesa one day . . ."

"Jorge, that's 'Laredo', not 'Lamesa'," J. R. corrected.

"Beggin' your pardon, Sarge," Jorge retorted. "But if we're not real careful, they'll be singin' that song about what happened to us, right here in Lamesa."

Despite Jorge's misgivings, Jim slipped into Sol Morris' room without being detected. He found papers in a trunk there, stuffed them in the front of his shirt, and left the room. The Rangers returned to camp where, after caring for their horses, they settled down to study the papers Jim had removed.

Two hours later, after the papers had been perused, Smoky half-whispered. "This proves it. It's all here. Payments. Instructions. Names. Dates. Everything. With this information, we can go after the head man now. Good thing Morris didn't trust him."

"It won't be quite that easy," J. R. protested. "We're talking about a mighty powerful *hombre* here. One with enough connections to get us all thrown outta the Rangers. Mebbe even enough influence to have us tossed in jail on some trumped up charge."

"No worries yet," Jim said. "We're not goin' after him, at least not quite now."

"Why not?" Jeff asked.

"Because, right now, with what we've got here we might be able to prove bribery or extortion, perhaps even conspiracy to commit robberies, but I want this man for more. I want to be able to arrest him for murder, and whoever is workin' for him, bet a hat on it."

Jim's eyes, cold and hard, like chips of blue ice, fixed every man in the tent.

"That especially goes for the men who got Kev. So we'll let things ride for a few days. Our man's not goin' anywhere, and I can telegraph Cap'n Trumbull to pick him up anytime. Let's be patient, and see what his outfit's next move is.

Now, I've had a long day. I don't know about the rest of you, but I'm dog-tired, and I'm gonna get some sleep."

"That sounds good," Smoky said. He turned the coal-oil lamp low, then stretched out on his bunk.

For the next four days, the Rangers held to their routine of guarding the construction crews and keeping an eye out for trouble. Except for some minor washouts caused by daily and violent afternoon thunderstorms, no reports of problems anywhere else along the Texas and Pacific system came in. Nerves stretched taut, they awaited the attack which was certain to come. None of them had been able to come up with any ideas what the plans Sol Morris had spoken of with his dying breaths might be.

On the fifth morning, Joe Tate strolled up as they were finishing breakfast.

"Today's the big day," he said casually as he poured a mug of coffee. "I'm sure glad the weather's finally cooperatin'."

"Why, Joe?" Jim asked. "What's so special?"

"Today's the day we take the first train over the trestle across the Double Mountain Fork," Tate said. "A lotta the men'll be ridin' on it, kind of a celebration. Bill Beedle's already gone out there to make sure of everything. He rode out last night, just to check the trestle one last time. He took Matt Thompson and Steve Parker along with him. I sure as heck dunno what he's so worried about. As you know, I've had two men watchin' that trestle night and day for the past week."

Jim jumped up so fast he spilled his coffee. "The trestle! That's it, I'd bet my hat on it."

"You're right, Jim. That has to be it," Smoky said.

"What are y'all talkin' about?" Tate questioned.

"The trestle at Double Mountain Fork," Jim replied. "They're gonna wreck the train there."

"Who's gonna wreck the train?" Tate demanded. "What the devil are you talkin' about?"

"There's no time to explain," Jim replied. "Joe, we'll need a fast train with a boxcar for our horses, and as of your men as you can round up. Find 'em as many horses and rifles as you can. Quick. There's no time to lose."

The urgency in Jim's voice erased any doubts Tate might have had.

"All right, Lieutenant," he said. "I'll have a locomotive and cars ready in fifteen minutes."

Tate raced out of the mess, shouting orders.

"Get your horses, men," Jim ordered. He ran out of the mess tent, heading for the corral.

An hour later and two miles shy of the Double Mountain Fork trestle, the train carrying the Rangers and Joe Tate's men slowed to a stop.

"This is as far as we can go without bein' seen," Tate explained. "I sure hope you're wrong about this, Lieutenant."

He and Jim hopped from the locomotive. The other Rangers, along with several shotgun-toting railroaders, had already stepped from a flatcar.

"That makes two of us, Joe," Jim replied. "Still, everything fits. I'll tell you more once this is over, but for now, just trust me. I wish we could've taken this train all the way to the river, but like you said, we can't chance bein' spotted. I figure those renegades'll blow the trestle the minute they see us, so we've got to keep that from happening."

Tate shrugged. "It's your hide, not mine." They reached the boxcar containing the horses, and Tate slid the door open. The horses crammed shoulder to shoulder inside whinnied their anxiousness to get free of the packed car.

"I'll have my men along as quick as I can. But they're railroad men, not cowboys. Most of 'em have never sat a horse. They'll never be able to keep pace with you Rangers. Won't be able to shoot as good either."

The horses were jumped out of the boxcar, then swiftly saddled and bridled.

"Remember," Jim hollered. "No shootin' until I give the order. Now, mount up and let's ride!"

When Jim and his men slid their lathered, blowing horses to a halt on an embankment overlooking the Double Mountain Fork, the first train to cross was edging toward the trestle, its whistle blowing triumphantly as railroaders cheered.

"We're too late!" Jeff hollered.

"Not yet, we're not." Jim's face was a mask of determination. "I'm gonna try and stop that train. Rest of you cover me. Hope Joe and his men ain't too slow gettin' here. We need every gun we can get."

He jabbed his heels into Sam's ribs, sending his gelding plunging down the bank.

As Jim raced toward the river, shouts and curses arose from the rim rock overlooking the swirling waters of the rain-swollen river. Several gunmen popped up from their hiding places and sent a volley of lead at the rider on the big paint. Sam squealed in pain when a bullet tore along his flank, and Jim grunted when one clipped the top of his right shoulder. Then Ranger guns thundered a deadly answer, driving the ambushers back into cover, with two of their number draped lifelessly over the rocks. A third man clutched his belly, doubled over, then toppled over the fallen tree he'd used for cover and slid fifty feet to a rock shelf below.

Down the tracks, railroaders dove for safety. One took a bullet through his left leg, but before another slug could find him, two of his comrades pulled him to safety behind the tender.

Jim pulled his Winchester from its boot and fired two shots in the direction of the ambushers.

Then, he ricocheted several rounds off the locomotive, driving the engineer from his throttle. The trainman shoved back the throttle, and as he and the fireman dove to the floor the train slowed to a halt.

"Stay down!" Jim shouted to the crew, as he raced alongside the engine. Behind him, J. R. Huggins yelped in pain. Jim turned to see him spin from Brazos' back. The gunman who'd hit Huggins drew a bead on Jim, but Jim's bullet tore into the renegade's chest and knocked him from his perch.

"Don't see Beedle anywhere," Jim muttered as Sam pounded up to the riverbank, where the bulk of the train sheltered them from the riflemen above. He pulled Sam to a stop and peered through the wooden supports of the trestle. Behind him, the crackle of rifle fire continued as the other Rangers bore down on the gunmen. Yelps of pain indicated more men were falling to the Rangers' accurate shooting. He just hoped none of those cries came from any of his men.

A slight movement far below caught Jim's eye. He realized it was Bill Beedle, who had just scratched a match to life, and now lit the fuse on a bundle of dynamite attached to one of the main support beams. That explosive would blast the trestle to pieces, sending the train and its passengers into the raging river and certain death.

"Don't, Beedle!" Jim shouted. He threw his

rifle to his shoulder, took aim, and fired a hasty shot. His bullet tore into the railroader's stomach. Beedle doubled over in pain from the impact of the slug, then dropped to the rocks. Seconds later, the dynamite exploded with a deafening roar. Under Sam's hooves the muddy riverbank, weakened from days of rain and high water, collapsed, sending horse and rider tumbling into the furious waters. They hit with a tremendous splash and disappeared under the roiling current.

Jim clung to the saddlehorn with a strength born of desperation as Sam sank beneath the water. His lungs were to the breaking point when his horse's hooves finally hit bottom and Sam rebounded toward the surface. Once his horse broke above the racing water, Jim kicked his feet from the stirrups and left the saddle. He held onto the horn and clung to the powerfully swimming paint. The current swept them along at a dizzying speed until Sam's hooves struck bottom along a gravel bar. The exhausted gelding lunged from the river, dragging Jim with him. Sam stood for a moment, spraddle-legged, head drooping. Jim lay unmoving. Sam nuzzled at him until he rolled onto his back.

Gasping and choking, Jim reached up to stroke Sam's velvety muzzle.

"No, pard, you're not gettin' any peppermints." His chuckle sounded weak, and a sharp pain shot through his right side. "Need to catch my breath, and I might've broken a rib. Let's just rest a minute or two." His hand dropped as he slipped into unconsciousness.

"Jim! Jim!"

Jim was roused by the voices calling him. He pushed himself to his feet. Once again pain ripped through his side.

"Down here!" he called. It was now almost full dark.

"Wonder how long I've been out, Sam?"

Sam responded with a soft nicker, and nuzzled Jim's cheek.

"Jim! Where the devil are you?" The voices were louder now.

"Over here!" Jim shouted.

A moment later, a lantern's light appeared along the riverbank. Red McGuire and Andre Miller came into view.

"Jim, there you are!" Red shouted. "We figured you were a goner, for certain."

"Well, I won't need a bath this Saturday, that's for sure." Jim chuckled, then sobered. "What happened at the trestle?"

"You Rangers stopped us just in time," Miller answered. "The trestle's mostly gone, but the train didn't go into the river."

"What about Beedle?"

"Far as we can tell, there's nothin' left of him," Red said. "Most of his men are dead. But I don't think any of your Rangers were killed. Couple of us railroaders were wounded, but I don't think too badly. Joe and his men are helpin' your pardners round up what's left of those renegades. How'd you know what Beedle was up to?"

"It's a long story, which'll have to wait," Jim replied. "You said none of my men were killed. What about J. R. Huggins? He got shot off his horse."

"I dunno," Miller admitted. "We haven't seen him. We were too busy tryin' to get to you."

"How do we get outta here?" Jim asked. "I've gotta see if J. R.'s all right."

"Just follow us," Red answered. "We came down on ropes, tryin' to get to you quick as possible, which sure wasn't easy, but there's a section of bank downstream you and your horse can climb. It'll be a scramble, but I think you can make it."

"Bet your hat I'll make it," Jim snapped. "Lead the way."

After climbing the bank, Jim was soon back at the train. Smoky and Jeff were guarding several prisoners, and to his relief, J. R. stood alongside them.

Smoky laughed. "Told you Jim'd never drown, Jeff. He's just too doggone ornery. Even the fishes don't want him."

Jim found that he could grin, too. "Where's Jorge?"

"Right behind you," Jorge called. "I was just makin' sure there's none of those coyotes who were still slinkin' through the rocks."

"Not to worry, Jorge, we got 'em all," J.R. said. "And one thing's for certain. Bill Beedle won't be usin' any more dynamite." He pointed to one of the prisoners. "That's Matt Thompson. He's ready to sing like a canary to save his skin."

Jim eyed the patch of crimson staining J. R.'s shirtfront.

"Never mind about Thompson," he said. "How about you, J.R.? You all right? I saw you get nailed and thought you were hit hard, the way you went outta the saddle. And why were you followin' me? I ordered all of you to stay behind and cover me."

"Nah, I didn't get hit too bad," J. R. answered, with a shrug. "Bullet just took off a hunk of flesh along my ribs. I'll be okay." He paused and looked at the bloody bullet rip in the shoulder of Jim's shirt. "But what about you? Looks like you took a slug."

"Only a crease," Jim said. "And you still didn't answer my question. Why'd you disobey my orders?"

J. R. shrugged. "Far as why I followed you, figured I could get a better angle at some of those drygulchers from down below. Good thing I did, too. One of 'em was about ready to put a bullet in your back. I got him first." He looked around, assessing the scene. "Guess it's all over but the cleanup."

"Yeah, here," Jim answered, his blue eyes blazing with anger. "But not back in Austin. Not by a long shot. And you can bet your hat on that."

CHAPTER FOURTEEN

"I'm sorry, sir, but you can't go in there. The Senate is in closed door session."

"This says I can," Jim snapped. He slid a folded document from his shirt pocket. "I've got a warrant here, which must be served. And I'm goin' in there even if I have to go through you to do so. Is that clear?"

Jim tapped the butt of his Colt for emphasis.

The guard at the door of the State Senate chambers hesitated. His gaze wavered to the warrant, to the Ranger badge on Jim's chest, and finally to Jim's determined face.

"I guess, I mean, uh, well, I think it should be all right," he stammered.

"There's nothing to think about," Jim growled. He pushed his way past the guard and into the chambers.

"Ranger, you'll have to wait," the sergeant at arms whispered, when Jim tried to push past him. "Senator Cox is speaking."

"Well, his speech is about to be cut short," Jim retorted. He pulled his gun from its holster. "You gonna try and stop me?"

The official gulped hard. "No, sir. You go right ahead, Ranger."

Jim brushed by the man and headed for the

podium, where Senator Thaddeus Cox stood. The senator's deep voice boomed throughout the chambers as he spoke. He had the other senators in rapt attention. None of them noticed the tall lawman who held a Colt in his left hand approaching Cox.

"And I say this proposed bill would be a disaster for the people of this great state of Texas!" he shouted, pounding his fist on the dais for emphasis. "I maintain, for the good of the entire Lone Star State, this bill must be defeated!"

Jim broke in, his voice restrained, but edged. "Fine speech, Senator. Very fine indeed."

The legislators turned to look for the source of the voice. A low murmur swept through the room as they noticed the grim-visaged Jim, who stood at the edge of the stage with his gun out and pointed directly at Cox.

"However, Senator, I'm afraid you won't be voting on any bill or anything else for a long time to come. Texas Ranger. Thaddeus Cox, I have here a warrant for your arrest on the charges of extortion, bribery, destruction of property, assault, attempted murder, several counts of murder, conspiracy to commit murder, accessory to murder. One of those murdered, as a matter of fact, was a young Texas Ranger. You'll hang for that, Senator."

"You will do no such thing!" Cox screamed. "Sergeant at Arms, remove this man from the chambers, and have him arrested. At once!"

"He can't help you, Senator. No one can." Jim's voice was edged steel. He climbed the stairs, his gun steady on Cox. "A lot of innocent people were hurt or killed because of you."

"Sergeant at Arms!" Cox screamed again, his voice breaking.

"Will you come along peaceably, Senator, or will I have to shoot you for resistin' arrest?" Jim asked. "Truthfully, nothin' would give me greater pleasure than to gut-shoot you right where you stand."

Cox regained his composure somewhat. "I'll . . . I'll surrender peaceably, Ranger," he managed to say. "However, I will have your badge for this. This is preposterous. It's a travesty. In fact, perhaps I will even introduce legislation to disband the Texas Rangers for this outrage!"

"Just shut up, and step over here, Senator."

"Certainly, Ranger." Cox's right hand dipped inside his coat as if to remove a handkerchief to wipe his sweating brow. He whipped out a .41 caliber Derringer, pulling the trigger as the little gun came to bear on where Jim should have been.

But Jim had anticipated Cox's treachery. He leaped to the side before the senator even pulled the trigger.

Cox's bullet whipped past Jim and plowed into the desk of the senator from Houston.

Jim, having maintained his aim on Cox, pulled

the trigger of his Colt and sent an ounce of lead slamming into the senator's ample belly.

Cox staggered momentarily, then tried to bring the little Derringer in line with Jim's head for his second bullet.

Jim fired again. His second slug smashed directly into Cox's heart. Dead on his feet, the senator swayed for a moment, his mouth gaping. He staggered sideways, and knocked the lectern over as he crumpled to the floor.

Jim walked over to Cox and kicked his Derringer out of reach.

"You made your choice, Senator," he said.

CHAPTER FIFTEEN

Captain Hank Trumbull glared fiercely at Jim Blawcyzk. "Lieutenant, I should bust you out of the Rangers for goin' ahead without checkin' with me first. If anything had gone wrong . . ." Trumbull left the rest of his thoughts unspoken.

"That's exactly why I didn't clear things with you first, Cap'n," Jim replied. They were in Trumbull's office at Ranger Headquarters. "This way, if anything had gone haywire, you could have claimed I was actin' on my own, without official sanction from headquarters. That would've kept the Rangers in the clear. Besides, I had plenty of evidence on Senator Cox. Judge Simon was more than happy to issue that warrant."

"The orders you gave me, Cap'n, were to find and stop whoever was out to destroy the Texas and Pacific Railroad," Jim said, with a grin. "That's just what I did."

"Don't get uppity with me, Lieutenant," Trumbull snapped. "I don't like it. Couple of state senators are callin' for an investigation."

"You want me to resign, Cap'n?"

Trumbull exploded. "What! You taken leave of your senses, Jim? Gone plumb crazy? I'm not worried about a couple of penny-ante politician cronies of Cox. That's enough of that kind of talk." He sat down and picked up Jim's report, which was lying on his desk.

"Okay. Let's start at the beginning."

"Sure, Cap'n," Jim answered. "I know it's pretty incredible. You see, with his bein' chairman of the Senate's transportation committee, Cox was able to obtain inside information on rail and road projects long before the information became public knowledge. When he found out the Texas and Pacific was planning a line from Abilene to Twist, then perhaps up into Colorado, he bought up most of the land along the proposed route, quiet-like. He used several accomplices to buy it for him under their names. We've still got to round up those men. Anyway, once Cox controlled most of the land along the right of way, he jacked the price sky-high. He never figured the T&P would look for an alternate route."

Trumbull nodded. "But they did."

"They did. In fact, they found a couple of 'em. They ended up rejectin' the one from Sweetwater, mostly because of the soils along that route bein' too sandy, which meant they'd have needed a lot more ballast for the roadbed. Plus, Big Spring offered the T&P some mighty powerful incentives to locate big freight yards there. There was nothing crooked about their offer. I checked into that. It was just smart business."

"So that's what put you onto Cox."

"Eventually, yes. I just couldn't figure out why the T&P would choose such a roundabout route to Twist. However, with Cox basically blackmailing the railroad, they decided to tell him to take his right-of-way land and go pound salt. Of course, once they did that, Cox's land was practically worthless, so he tried his darndest to get the Legislature to void the Texas and Pacific's franchise. When that didn't work, he decided to ruin the railroad. He bribed Sol Morris and Bill Beedle into workin' for him. Being the chief operating men for the building of the spur to Twist, they were in the perfect position to sabotage the construction. They went about everything real smart, too. Didn't rush things, even after us Rangers were on the scene."

"What about the wrecked train you were on?"

"That was just an unlucky coincidence. I was in the wrong place. However, that turned out to be a lucky break for us."

Jim paused, then continued. "I hate to say this, but it was another lucky break for us when Cox tried to down me and I had to plug him."

"How's that?"

"Because I'm not sure we could have convicted him. I wanted to take Beedle alive, so I'd have at least one witness against Cox. Too bad I drilled him dead center."

Trumbull chuckled. "Better'n him drillin' you dead center," he said. "Besides, it seemed like

Beedle wanted to die, rather'n facin' a noose. He had to purposely light that fuse close to the dynamite when he set it off."

"True on both counts," Jim agreed. "And between the papers we found in Morris' and Beedle's stuff, plus the testimony of Matt Thompson, we should have had enough evidence to get a conviction. Still, Cox had influence and powerful friends. And he would have hired the slickest lawyers in Texas. He just might have gotten off."

"Well, Jim, you did a good job," Trumbull praised. "Why don't you take a few days off and get some rest? Let those wounds heal up a little more."

"I'm doin' just fine, Cap'n," Jim said. "Ready to ride."

"You're not foolin' me," Trumbull said. "I can tell by the way you're movin' those wounds are still botherin' you. You're one of the toughest *hombres* I've ever known, Jim, but no one's indestructible, and I'd sure hate to lose you by sendin' you out too soon, before you're healed up. Let someone else take the next job."

Trumbull picked up several letters. "Besides," he continued, "I've gotten quite a few complaints about a certain palomino paint cayuse. Seems Sam's been chompin' on livery stable hostlers again."

"Hey, I warn those *hombres* not to go near Sam,

just to throw his feed in the stall," Jim protested.

Trumbull chuckled. "I know. But mebbe we should give those hostlers a few days' rest, too. Go on home, Ranger."

Jim smiled. "Julia and Charlie'll sure appreciate that, Cap'n. Besides, I've got to hang around town for a few days in any event. James Reasoner and Chet Dobson'll get here on the noon train tomorrow. I promised them a full report. Smoky, Jorge, Jeff, and J. R. will be arrivin' on the same train, along with the prisoners we took. We still have a few loose ends to tie up."

Jim sighed. "I suppose we'll never know for certain which one of Cox's hired guns killed Kevin Smith, but we figure it must've been one of the gang we fought it out with at the Double Mountain Fork. Most of 'em were wiped out, and we captured the rest. With Thaddeus Cox dead, and the others facin' a noose for sure, Kev can rest easy."

"Which is all that matters," Trumbull replied. He closed the folder which contained Jim's report.

"I'll see you tomorrow, Jim."

"*Hasta la Vista*, Cap'n. See you *manana*."

A few moments later, Jim was in the saddle. He pointed Sam toward home and kicked him into a lope, heading for a joyous reunion with his wife and son.

About the Author

James J. Griffin, although a native New Englander, is a lifelong horseman, Western enthusiast, and amateur historian of the Texas Rangers. His large collection of Texas Ranger artifacts is now in the permanent collections of the Texas Ranger Hall of Fame and Museum. Jim has traveled extensively throughout the western United States and Canada, and his research has taken him to many of the famous Old West towns, such as Tombstone, Deadwood, Cheyenne, Pecos, and many others. While Jim's books are fiction, he does try to keep them as historically accurate as possible within that realm. Jim's books are traditional Westerns in the best sense of the term, with strong, moral heroes. Most of his novels are suitable for almost all ages.

When not writing, Jim can almost always be found in the saddle. He is a member of Western Writers of America and Western Fictioneers. He divides his time between Branford, Connecticut and Keene, New Hampshire, when not out West.

To learn more about Jim, visit his website at www.jamesjgriffin.net.

Acknowledgements

Thanks to Texas Ranger Sergeant Jim Huggins of Company A, Retired, The Texas Ranger Hall of Fame and Museum in Waco, and Karl Rehn and Penny Riggs of KR Training, Manheim, Texas.

Also my thanks to an excellent editor, Charlie Whipple.

Books are produced in the United States using U.S.-based materials

Books are printed using a revolutionary new process called THINKtech™ that lowers energy usage by 70% and increases overall quality

Books are durable and flexible because of smythe-sewing

Paper is sourced using environmentally responsible foresting methods and the paper is acid-free

Center Point Large Print
600 Brooks Road / PO Box 1
Thorndike, ME 04986-0001 USA

(207) 568-3717

US & Canada:
1 800 929-9108
www.centerpointlargeprint.com